Hawk's Bounty

Haven MC
Book Two

by Carson Mackenzie

CM Books, LLC

Published by CM Books, LLC
Copyright © Dec 2016 Carson Mackenzie
Cover Design by Carson Mackenzie
ISBN# 978-1-952184-23-9

CM Books, LLC

Synopsis

Kaden "Hawk" Cross is used to being in control of every aspect of his life: from his short stint in the military to his VP position in the Haven MC. But when he meets a woman who threatens his control, he is reminded why he never makes rash decisions—they tend to come back and bite you.

Charlie Rhoades is a woman who has always gone after what she wants. And taking a job across the country that would give her the opportunity to look for the grandfather she never met made sense. What didn't make sense? Is finding a man who heats her blood but seems totally aloof toward her. But being a bounty hunter, she isn't easily deterred by his actions; she is more apt to be assertive. Good for her, not so much for the biker who would rather be the pursuer.

On the outside, Haven MC is the typical motorcycle club filled with bikers—on the inside, they are men with the knowledge and abilities to keep not only their club safe but their country. Missions come and go, but what keeps the men of Haven committed, is the unwavering Brotherhood and the acceptance from the women who cross their paths.

CM Books, LLC

Table of Contents

CM Books, LLC

CM Books, LLC

Prologue

Hawk

"Hey, asshole! You need to park your bike somewhere else."

I turned off my bike and undid the snap on my chin strap before I acknowledged the young guy who stood in front of my bike. Not that I was old by any means, but somedays I felt like it.

"Why? You own this spot?" I asked, then dismounted my bike, pulled the helmet off and set it on the seat, not once taking my eyes off the guy.

"Smart guy, huh? These spots are reserved for Haven MC. So why don't you move along."

I looked the guy over; average height, stocky build. After being in the military, it was second nature to size a person up and access the threat level. I also knew about the motorcycle club he was referring to, I grew up here, and the Haven MC had always been around. The guy was probably a prospect with the club and his job was to keep an eye on the row of bikes I parked beside.

"I'm no genius, but my IQ is above average." At the guy's blank look, I smirked. "I would move, but I'm thirsty and hungry, and this place sells bo..." I didn't finish my sentence because when I went to step around him, he placed a hand on my forearm.

"I won't tell you again, asshole. If you know what's good for you, you'll move the bike. Better yet, find some other place to eat."

I looked down at his hand, then back at him. Messing with the guy had been a little entertaining, now—not so much. "Know what will be good for you? Removing your damn hand if you want to keep the use of it."

The guy stiffened, glared at me, then dropped his hand. Before he could reply, the door to the place opened and several men dressed like the guy in front me, in leather vests, walked out. They stopped and looked between him and me.

The biggest of the men stepped forward, and the vest he wore was covered in patches. The one that grabbed my attention read President. When I looked at him, I found myself pinned by green eyes while he spoke to his man, "Gotta problem, Prospect?"

I'd been right on my initial assessment and bet if the guy who tried to stop me from entering were to turn around, his vest would have 'Prospect' written across the back of the otherwise plain vest.

"No, Prez. Nothing I can't handle. I was telling this dickhead that he needed to move along when he pulled in and parked beside the bikes as if he had a right."

10

The prez, as the prospect called him, shook his head and took a deep breath. "You got a problem with us?" he asked me.

"Does it make a difference?" I asked, and he smirked.

"Son, it does when you give one of my men shit," he said, and the men behind him chuckled.

Damn, I was tired and hungry and not looking for trouble. I might have been gone from the area for a while, but it didn't mean I'd forgotten that Haven pretty much ran the town. I looked at the men and wondered if this went south, how many I could deal with before they overpowered me. The stocky prospect was close enough to throat punch before the others got the opportunity to move. That would leave the president and the four men behind him. Even with twenty years or more in age, the president was in shape and had three inches on me and a good thirty pounds. Out of the other four bikers, two looked as if they'd be close to the president's age. The other two were showing more wear and tear on them and seemed to be significantly older than the others.

"Maybe he's spying for another club. He seems to have a problem with respect, Prez. Want me to give him a lesson?" the prospect asked.

I cut my eyes to the prospect and smirked. "Paranoid much?" Geez, the idiot was going to be the cause of my ass getting handed to me.

"You got no idea," was said from one of the other men and the comment had the president turning his head and looking at him.

"Enough, Smoke."

"Sorry, Prez."

"Where you from, boy? Haven't seen you around here." The old man that spoke stepped from behind the president.

I ignored the 'boy' and accepted the man meant nothing by it since he looked like he could be someone's grandpa. "Born and raised."

The president frowned. "Never seen you in town before."

"Don't live in town." I shrugged.

The man tilted his head to the side and frowned while he stared at me. I wasn't sure what the man was looking for, so I stared back. After a minute, he nodded as if he agreed with whatever he saw.

"Enjoy your food. The Roadhouse has the best steaks and burgers in town."

"Yeah? Good, because when it was Lester's place the food was barely tolerable." I had no clue what was with the big man or the shift in the atmosphere from minutes ago. And then I wondered if I should be worried or not.

He smirked. "You must not have been back in town long; this place hasn't been Lester's for a few years," he said.

"Yeah," was all I replied. They didn't need to know I only been back less than a week. I'd spent time riding across the country to clear my head of the military and prepare to come home for the first time since I buried my parents two years ago.

12

"After you eat, why don't you come by the clubhouse. Ask for Prez or Wild Bill at the gate." The man lifted his chin toward the bikes, then turned with the others to head toward them. Before he took two steps, he stopped and turned his head in my direction. "Ya gotta name, son?"

"Kaden. Kaden Cross."

"See you later, Cross."

"You know something I don't? I didn't say yes to your invitation," I said and stepped up to the door of the Roadhouse.

"No, you didn't," the president said and threw his leg over his bike.

I reached for the handle on the door as I watched the men get on their bikes. Curiosity got the better of me and I had to ask, "Why did you give the invite?"

There was a long pause before he answered, "Just a hunch. If you decide you want to take me up on my offer— ask inside for directions to the clubhouse." The bikes started up and the president gave me a two-finger salute as he pulled out with the other men following.

I stood there for a moment, then shook my head and pulled the door open. I was intrigued, but was it enough to take the man up on his offer?

Throwing cash down on the table to cover the food and tip, I walked out of the establishment and mounted my bike. With my stomach full, I looked up at the sky that was turning to dusk. I sighed, pulled my helmet on, cranked my bike, then started out of the lot. When I reached the edge of

13

the parking lot, a right turn would lead me back in the direction to my house. Instead, I turned left and pulled back on the throttle.

Guess the intrigue had won.

Ten minutes and several turns later, I pulled up in front of a gate. I hadn't needed any directions to the Haven clubhouse. If you lived in a thirty-mile radius, you knew exactly where the club was located.

"You got business here?" A biker asked as he stepped out of the shack on the other side of the fencing. This one was tall, thin, and I noticed his skin was a little pasty even in the fading light of the day. He wore a plain vest, which meant he was another prospect for the club.

"Here to see Wild Bill," I said and eyed the man. If he wasn't using, I'd sign my bike over. He sniffed, and I'd bet it had nothing to do with a running nose and everything to do with snorting some type of powder.

The lot behind the gate was filled with bikes and men. The building looked decent size from where I sat, and if the bikers didn't let me know I was at the right place, the skull emblem with Haven MC circling it would have. Music filled the air with loud voices and laughter along with the strong smell of weed.

Focused on the parking lot, I missed the other man who stepped out of the shack until he spoke, "That so? What's your business with Prez?"

I looked at the new man, and the first thing I noticed was the difference in the two men's vest. This man's vest held patches on the front like the men from earlier along with one that read Sergeant at Arms.

I must have taken too long to answer, at least by his estimation, because he asked, "You got a hearing problem? I asked you a question, boy."

I lifted a brow and stared at the man and mulled over in my head if my interest in why Wild Bill invited me to the clubhouse outweighed my annoyance of how the asshole in front of me said 'boy.' The tone he used wasn't the same as how the older biker from earlier said the word.

Annoyance won, and as I opened my mouth to confront the nosy bastard, "Let the man in, Jacks!" Wild Bill yelled as he crossed the lot toward the gate, drawing my attention to him.

Jacks curled his lip at me, then turned toward Wild Bill. "I was fixin' to, Prez, as soon as he told what business he had with you."

Wild Bill's brows scrunched together as he looked at Jacks. "Open the damn gate." The prospect pulled a lever and rolled the gate open. It didn't go unnoticed that it was done after Jacks jerked his chin toward it.

I eased through the gate and Wild Bill waved his arm in the direction where the other bikes were parked. "Find a spot, Kaden, and I'll meet you at the door."

"Sure thing." I found a spot at the end of a row of bikes and backed my bike up again the fence. As I walked to the front of the clubhouse, I felt eyes on me from some of the bikers who were standing around and wondered if this had been the best idea.

"Not something for you to be concerned, Stone," Wild Bill said to a biker who stood beside him at the door as I walked up.

The biker Wild Bill called Stone glanced at me, then looked back at Wild Bill. "Nowadays seems like a lot of things going on in the club without clearing it through the voting members. As VP, I should be informed on what's going on. Some of the members have concerns that Haven is changing and they ain't sure they like it."

"Yeah, you might be the VP, but last time I looked at my vest, I wear the President's patch. What I think is a lot of folks forget whose club this actually is."

I watched the VP's body stiffen as he glared at Wild Bill. Wild Bill stared back and raised his eyebrows at the VP. As I stood there and took in the interaction between the men, I wondered what kinda problems Haven had considering the top two men in the club seemed at odds.

"Oh, they know. Some just don't agree with it," the VP said and turned and walked off. If I hadn't been watching the president's reaction, I would have missed the slight jerk of his head. When I glanced over my shoulder, two men who were standing in a small group close by, nodded and walked off.

"Come on, Cross. Let's go to my office and talk." Wild Bill didn't wait for me to respond, he pulled the door open and walked inside. I followed, my interest in the president growing the more I was around him.

Inside held more people enjoying the party and the music was much louder inside than outside. Wild Bill

16

stopped at the entrance to a huge open room filled with men and women barely dressed. He made a hand gesture at the man standing behind a bar in the corner. When the man acknowledged him with a chin lift, Wild Bill started walking again. After a turn down a short hallway and past a few doors, we reached his office and he pulled out keys and unlocked the door.

Once inside, he motioned me to one of the chairs that sat in front of his desk. I glanced around the large room. A table with chairs around it was off to one side, and on the other side, a couch was against the wall. As I sat, Wild Bill did the same behind his desk. Before either of us said a word there was a knock on the door.

"Enter," Wild Bill yelled and the man from behind the bar walked in carrying two beers. He handed one to Wild Bill, and I noticed a 'Prospect' patch on the back of his vest, too, then he handed the other beer to me.

"Thanks, man," I said as I reached for the bottle.

"No problem. Anything else, Prez," the man said on his way to the door.

"Nah, Skid, we're good for now."

As the prospect walked out, I twisted the top off the bottle and took a drink of my beer while I waited for Wild Bill to do the same.

He leaned back in his chair and studied me for a minute before he spoke, "How long you been out of the military?"

I hadn't expected him to lead with that particular question and though it caught me off guard somewhat, I

17

didn't allow it to show on my face. "Figure not as long as you."

Wild Bill's head tilted back, and his laugh was deep and loud. When he looked back at me, he smiled. "I'd agree with you there. What branch did you serve in?"

"Army. You?"

"Same."

I nodded. And since I wasn't one to hold back my thoughts, I asked, "Going to tell me what I'm doing here?"

"Yeah, in due time. What'd you specialize in?"

"MI." Wild Bill tilted his head to the side, then sat forward and leaned his elbows on the desk.

"Military Intelligence. Were you good at it?"

I smirked. "Guess it depends on who you ask?"

"Well, you don't lack for brains, considering MI's come out of the top two percent of personnel. But I am curious as to why you got out?"

I frowned at the man who I didn't really know and wondered how much information I wanted to share. "Let's just say I don't accept failure."

I saw the understanding in Wild Bill's eyes. He may not have known exactly what my circumstance was, but I imagine he had dealt with some of his own. And I had every reason to believe Haven MC was a problem for him or at the very least a nuisance. He was right, I didn't lack for smarts, and from the little I'd witness so far, I would guess internal club problems was creating issues between his members.

"You couldn't have served more than six or eight years. Men with your training and specialty usually stay in

18

until retirement, or if they do leave, it's to pursue a career in one of the government agencies. Must have been something big that happened to make you leave the military and bypass a lucrative career elsewhere in the same field."

I ran a hand over the day-old growth of hair on my face and debated if I wanted to share what had happened that left a bad taste in my mouth for a job I had enjoyed.

"Sometimes it helps to talk about it. Sometimes it doesn't," Wild Bill said and shrugged.

With my decision made, I took a long drink of my beer. "I was on my third rotation to the Middle East. The MI's were stationed in tents on top of a knoll where we could receive intel and also collect our own from the satellites our computers were programmed into. Every bit of intel was then pieced together so we could give the frontline units the best possible advantage. Wrong intel or the wrong analysis of the situation could cost lives.

"I left the military after my enlistment at the end of my tour because the green Captain they sent my team thought he was the best. He blew off the assessment I made on the battalion's chance of intercepting the enemy before they had a chance to dig in and set up at the new location they were headed to. The Captain argued with me and told me I was reading one of the reports wrong. He felt the enemy wasn't going to move and if they did, it would be to another location. One the Captain said he would bank on," I stopped explaining and took another drink.

"He overrode you," Wild Bill said, but it wasn't a question.

"Yes. He disagreed with me, though the other three who analyzed the material with me, agreed with my assessment. Twenty-three men died, and dozens were wounded. And when it was time to answer for it, he told the higher powers that he stood by his own assessment because any intel had a percentage of error. I called bullshit and was told that loss of life is calculated into every maneuver. The Captain got a slap on the wrist, and I lost my taste for MI. Twenty-three men died because we failed them. His arrogance with the thought that he was the best," I barely spoke the last two sentences above a whisper.

"You mentioned you were from around here." I nodded, appreciating the rapid change in subject with no questions on the previous one. "How long have you been back in the area?"

"Not long. After my discharge I traveled across the US, dealing with a few issues."

"Yeah? What happened to give you those issues?"

With my greatest failure shared, I asked, "Why the interest in me? You just met me a couple hours ago. Know nothing about me other than I'm from around here and ex-military because my team failed the men who we were supposed to protect. For all you know, I could be one crazy motherfucker."

Wild Bill smirked. "It wasn't your team's failure; it was one officer's who should've listened to his team. Besides, you wouldn't be the first one Haven has. Hell, you'd be lucky to be considered in the top five for that title. Haven MC isn't short on peculiar. I like to refer to it as eccentric. However,

20

what we are lacking? Is trust and loyalty. Men that know right from wrong. Or at the least care about it. Don't misunderstand me, Haven has over the years been involved in things that weren't remotely close on the legal side. Those times were under my grandfather and then my dad. But what I want for this club now, is more—I want every member to be proud to be a part of Haven. Right now though, the club has a cancer that has been growing over the years. I want to cut it out. Then when we get healthy, I've got a plan to make the club lucrative without stepping over the lines of the law." He chuckled, "At least not that far over. But I can't begin my new venture until I've recruited men I can trust to help me clean Haven up. Men with the same mindset I have."

"And you think I could be one of those men?" I pointed the bottle in the direction of the door. "Outside that door you have more than enough men in this MC. If you can't trust them or they aren't loyal to the club, why keep them around? Like you said outside, your club."

"I think you are exactly what I'm looking for. And if ridding the club of troublemakers was what I was after, they would have been booted already, but I want to make sure that I get every one of them out. Plus, I want to know exactly what they've been up to before I cut them out. My dad was killed on a run, and I want the ones responsible."

My eyebrows went up in surprise, then I frowned at Wild Bill. "If none of the men in Haven will help you, why the hell are you allowing *any* of the bastards to be a part of this club?"

"I've got plenty of backing in this club, Cross. Especially the older ones. Problem is, the ones responsible for my dad's death are members of Haven. And I want them. Them and everyone they're associated with, too."

I raise my hand and run it across the back of my neck. The military intelligence training in me pushing forward, wanting to locate the information needed to help Wild Bill. As I sat and drank my beer, Wild Bill sat quietly, letting me work out what he was asking of me.

"If...and I mean if I were to join your club. How are you going to bring me in without raising questions?"

"You'll prospect just like any other man who wants to be a part of the club. I don't expect this to be an easy task. Haven MC has been on the downslide for a while, it's gonna take time. I need men who have no problem putting in the effort. Roach will be your sponsor. You unofficially met him at the Roadhouse. He's ex-military and has been in this club since he turned eighteen. The only time he left, it was to serve his country."

"I know enough about clubs to know prospects get stuck with crappy jobs. Gathering information is easy. Just don't know how you expect me to be much help when I'm busy filling a prospect's role," I said and cocked a brow.

Wild Bill chuckled. "They do deal with shit no one else wants to do. But they also see and hear more than most members because they are always around. Being constantly in the background, the others tend to overlook prospects." Wild Bill pulled out his phone and quickly sent a text, then set it down. "Skid will bring us another round."

I nodded and tipped the beer and finished it off, then set the empty bottle on the desk. While we waited for the prospect to bring us fresh bottles, Wild Bill talk about his time in the military and the men he served with. By the time he finished, Skid knocked on the door with our drinks. When the door shut as he left, Wild Bill looked at me. "Well, you interested?"

I twisted the top off the bottle and held it out toward him. "Guess you're looking at Haven's newest prospect."

"To a new beginning for Haven MC," Wild Bill said and touched my beer bottle with his.

CM Books, LLC

Chapter One

Hawk

The hot shower felt good, but my couch felt even better. It had been a long week clearing out Katie's condo so the owner could start the repairs. The stairs were torn out and replaced with a portable staircase, leaving the furniture in the bedrooms, the only things that had to stay until the new stairs were built. No chance in hell the temp steps would take any weight over a normal size person going up and down them. Hell, it had gotten dicey a few times when two of us met in the middle.

I was glad we finished the task, and it had nothing to do with the labor. It had been hell working with Charlie every day. The more time I spent with her, the more I wanted her. It didn't help that every time she bent over to pick something up my dick hardened. Manual labor with a hard-on was definitely not something I would recommend.

With Prez and Keg headed to Black Hawk MC, I would be left in charge. When they got back, we were leaving

25

for a job in Boston. I so needed that distance from a certain redhead.

Right now, though, food, beer, and sleep were on my agenda. Or maybe the clubhouse and one of the hang-arounds to fuck would work, too. Better yet, drinking until I couldn't think. I got up and headed for the kitchen as the doorbell rang.

"Fuckin' A." I turned back the way I came and opened the door expecting to see one of my brothers standing on the other side. Instead, it was the woman who had recently taken up permanent residence in my head and had me jacking off like a teenage boy when I'd couldn't control my need for release.

"What are you doing here?" I asked harshly.

"Wow, you're welcoming. I brought food," Charlie said and held out a pizza box. I took the box and stepped back so she could enter.

"And why are you bringing pizza to my house?"

"I didn't find out until today that you actually lived in the same neighborhood so... You eat, don't you?" That was a damn loaded question. She'd run and hide if I told her all the things I wanted to do to her.

"Yeah, I eat." We walked into my living room, and I sat the pizza box on the coffee table. "Wanna beer to go with it?"

"Beer would be great." I went to the kitchen, grabbed the beer and a stack of napkins, then headed back into the living room. Charlie had taken a seat on the couch and sat

26

down beside her, making sure to leave enough space between us.

After I grabbed a slice of pizza and took a bite, Charlie turned to me.

"Do you have a steady woman?"

With my mouth full, I turned and looked at her, then shook my head.

"Good, then I don't have to feel guilty when I let you fuck me." Charlie watched me as her mouth closed around the end of the pizza slice she held in her hand.

I finished chewing the bite in my mouth before I answered her, "No one should feel guilty about fucking." I could feel her eyes on me as I continued to eat.

A few minutes passed in silence, and it made me wonder if she expected me to drop the pizza and go at her. Not as if I'd never done that before, but it was on my terms.

"Glad you agree. I love sex. It's hard finding a man who isn't threatened by a woman being upfront with what she needs and when she needs it. I like the looks of you, and damn, your body probably has most women, who come in contact with you, getting more than a little damp in their panties."

As I chewed, I cut my eyes to her. "Yours damp?" I asked and continued to eat as I waited for her to answer. I expected a bold comeback from her. If I learned anything in the short time I'd known her, it was that she was strong, smart, and liked to be in control, especially in her life.

"Guess you'll find out for yourself after we finish eating." She finished with the slice she was currently eating and then picked up her beer, drinking until the bottle was half empty. When she sat the bottle down on the table, I popped the last bit of crust in my mouth and turned toward her. The smile on her face told me that she was used to getting her way.

I didn't reply to her right then. Instead, I reached out, snagged her thighs, turning her to face me, and pulled her closer. One hand moved behind her neck to bring her face closer to mine, and I leaned down until our lips were damn near touching while my other hand slid up the inside of one of her thighs. I could feel the heat of her radiating through the material of her jeans, and I groaned inwardly because I knew if I stripped her down, she would be hot and wet, and ready for my touch.

Sliding my hand the rest of the way, I cupped her over her jeans and ran my fingers up and down the seam. I pressed down slightly with every pass. Charlie leaned in to close the space between our lips but, instead of letting them touch, I wrapped my fingers in her hair and pulled her head back.

By the widening of her eyes, I knew she was shocked at the move. With one last pass of my fingers between her legs, I removed my hand, let loose of her hair with the other one, and leaned away until I was sitting back on the couch. That's when I responded to her previous statement.

"Yeah, you are wet. Hot, too. You better go home and change those panties. I would hate for you to get chafed. Appreciate the pizza." I stood, picked up the box and the beer bottles off the coffee table, then headed toward the kitchen to throw them in the garbage.

"What the fuck! Are you kidding me? You walk away from a willing woman. Damn, are you into men? Is that it? Or are you just an asshole? Fuck this. It doesn't matter. I don't do games, dickhead. Your loss."

When I walked out of the kitchen, it took everything in me to steel my expression from her ranting, but the look on her face had my lips twitching. She stood at the front door mad, and the expression on her face showed only a mild case of shock that she wasn't getting her way.

"Charlie." She sneered but didn't reply, so I continued, "I don't play games either. And I'm glad you enjoy sex because when I have you, it is going to be in every way possible, and on my terms. Hope your stamina is up to par, sugar."

"I see asshole is the winning term for you!" Charlie yelled and threw open the door, then slammed it shut behind her.

I smirked and as I walked back into the living and flopped down on the couch, I burst into laughter. Growing up, I always like to play with fire. When I stared into the flames the flickering relaxed something inside me. Maybe it was the look but don't touch, or I could be burned factor that I enjoyed. I had a feeling I was going to find out because Charlie was going to be my new flame. I just hoped she didn't burn me to ashes.

Charlie

CM Books, LLC

"And men accuse women of being cock teasers." I pulled my bike into the garage, and by the time the door made it down, I was stomping my way into the house. I slammed the door, locked it, and reset the alarm.

"What an f'n prick!" I yelled into the emptiness as I reached the living room and grabbed the remote and turned on the TV. After, I went back into the kitchen, snagged the open bottle of wine and a glass, then went back to the living room and curled up on the end of the couch. Once the cork was pulled out of the bottle and I filled the glass, I drank the wine down and then filled the glass again before I sat the bottle on the table and picked up my cell phone. After I had scrolled through my contacts, I tapped on the name I wanted and listened to the phone ring.

"Hey, Charlie. What are you up to?" Katie answered, and her chirper voice had me grinding my teeth. But Moose never turned Katie down!

"That man is an arrogant ass," I jumped right in not giving Katie time to catch up. "If Moose is half as bad, I don't know how you put up with him. Acted like he was interested, then turns into a dick when confronted. Yeah, see if I feed his ass and go to him again. His terms. Sure, we see about that, the asshat." I kept going, and Katie listened until I ran out of steam. I knew I was acting irrationally, but I didn't give two shits. The man pissed me off.

"Sweetie, who are we talking about?"

"Hawk. Were you not listening to anything I said?" I asked, and Katie chuckled.

"Yes, I was listening to you, but you never mentioned who. What happened?" Katie asked, and then I heard a muffled "stop it," and it instantly brought me back to sane Charlie when I realized I just ranted like a crazy woman because I was turned down.

"Did I interrupt something?" I asked even knowing I probably was. Katie and Moose were sickeningly together. The man was unable to keep his hands off Katie, and I was unable to get a man to put his hands on me. Ugh!

"No, we just came to bed." Katie was too sweet.

Her response told me differently. "Thanks for lying so I wouldn't feel worse. Now go get lucky. Someone should have an enjoyable night."

"Charlie, if you need to talk, Moose can wait."

"It's okay. I actually feel better letting the crazy out. We can talk later. Go enjoy your man."

"Are you going to be okay?"

"Yes, I'm good. Now go, get down to business." Katie laughed, and we said our goodbyes and hung up. There was no reason for two of us to go to sleep sexually frustrated.

I sat my cell phone on the table, and the folder sitting off to the side drew my attention. I picked it up and pulled the picture out of the young man who laid on a bunk with his head propped up on his hand and dog tags hanging down from his neck. My grandfather. In the black and white photo his hair was dark, and I couldn't tell the color of his eyes, but my grandmother had told me he had black hair and I shared his green eyes. Other than the color of my eyes, I looked just like my grandmother. Her hair was deep red just as mine

31

was, but her eyes dark brown like the most sumptuous chocolate.

The photo was the only one that survived the fire that destroyed the house where she and my dad had lived in Chicago. Even with the frayed edges, a few water spots, and the natural aging of the photo, Travis said it was still in good shape and he had a contact that could help. I didn't ask who or how I was just thankful the man had made a copy of the photo and was working on finding out the name of the man in it. A picture, and what little information I had on him, came from a woman who suffered a stroke and whispered the only things she could remember of the man from her past.

After putting the picture away, I poured the last of the wine in my glass and tried to relax while focusing on the TV. It had lasted a whopping hour before Hawk worked his way back in. I would have gone for a long ride if I hadn't doused my bitchiness with wine. Instead, I went to my room and changed into yoga pants and a tank, grabbed my e-reader, then planted myself back on the couch. My cell rang no sooner than I open the book I had been reading.

I smiled when I saw who was calling and hit the button, "How is my best guy?"

"Doing good. How is my best girl?" My dad asked, and we both laughed. We started each phone call like that since I moved from Chicago to Maryland, and now Washington.

"You first. How is the job going, Dad? Working anything interesting?"

My dad had done twelve years in the Army right out of high school. When he exited the military, he went to work for the Chicago PD.

"No, but I wanted to share some news. I made Captain and looks like I'll be moving precincts and taking over the 9th."

"That's awesome, Dad. Congratulations! I wish I were there to celebrate with you and Mom. Does Fiona know you are going to be in the same precinct as her?" Fiona O'Malley and I grew up together. She was my best friend, even now with the miles between us.

"No, thought I would surprise her. My promotion has been announced; they just haven't shared that I'll be taking the spot at the 9th. Rosen is retiring for medical reasons, so it will happen pretty fast."

"Sorry to hear about Rosen. I always liked him. But Fiona will be thrilled to have you there, Dad. You know that."

"Yeah, it will be interesting if nothing else. So, how's the job going there? Ready to come back to Chicago?" My dad was good at making me smile.

"I think I will give it a little more time since I've only technically been working at it for a week."

"If you insist. Can't fault a dad from trying to get his little girl back home."

"There's no bounty hunting in Illinois, whatever would I do there?" I waited for it to come because Sean Rhoades liked his family close. And since my grandmother died, it only left him, myself and my mom. Maybe a

33

grandfather if he was still alive. I knew my dad wouldn't mention anything about that being one of the reasons for the relocation. He knew less about his dad than I did.

"You would make a great cop, Charlie." I heard my mom in the background telling him to stop harassing me. He and I had been over that subject a hundred times. His muffled, "Please, like she listens," made me chuckle. "Love ya, baby girl. Here's your mom." Before I could reply, he was gone, and my mom had taken over the phone.

"Now, how are you and have you met any decent eligible men there?" My mom, Libby, was great, but the woman was relentless on me finding that special person to share my life with, but I knew her too well to fall into her trap.

"So how are Serena and Milana?"

"Don't think you are going to get out of answering me by changing the subject. My friends are fine. Now stop hedging and give your old mother the skinny."

"Mom, please don't say that again." I laughed. "Besides, you are not old." Mom hadn't met my dad until after he started working for the police department. They had met at a policemen's ball, and both said it was love at first sight.

"Who is he? And don't say it is one of the brothers you are working with," she whispered, and that told me my dad was still close by.

"It is not one of the guys. Though they are hot, I still wouldn't go there. And there is no he for me. I've only been here a month, Mom," I said, and the voice in the back of my mind shouted "liar, liar" so I slammed that door shut. No way was I going to get into all that was Kaden Cross with my mother.

"Okay, don't tell me. But I can't help it if I want the same for you as I have with your dad."

My parents never hid their love for each other. Between the smallest of touches, the kisses shared, and the way they looked at each other, no one could miss their connection. As a kid, I remember feeling embarrassed when friends were over; as a young woman, that feeling changed to envy and hope that I would have what they shared.

"I know, Mom. But sometimes it's complicated."

"Charlie, I'm not going to push you to open up to me, but can I give a little advice?"

"Sure, Mom." I grinned. As if the woman wouldn't share her advice even if I told her I didn't want to hear it.

"You're a strong woman who knows exactly what she wants and goes for it. You've been like that since you were little. But, honey, sometimes letting go and allowing someone else to take over isn't a bad thing, especially if that someone is special and wants to take care of you, not change you. There's nothing wrong with that, Charlie."

"I guess I'm worried I'll lose myself along the way, Mom. I've worked hard to get where I am," I whispered as Kaden's face flashed behind my eyes.

"Oh, honey, every relationship is give and take. Sometimes you just got to take the chance and have enough trust in the man to not hurt you. In every relationship there has to be some compromising if you want it to last."

35

"Thanks, Mom. Love you."

"Love you, too, Charlie. It's late, I better let you go. Call me soon, honey."

"I will. Tell, Dad, congrats again and that I love him. Bye, Mom."

After she had said goodbye, I disconnected the call, leaned my head back on the couch, and let Kaden float through. Was he worth the risk?

Chapter Two

Hawk

Lifting my chin to the prospect at the gate, I pulled up to the clubhouse. After I backed my bike into an open space in the row of others, I dismounted and headed in. The voices coming from the kitchen told me where I would find my brothers.

"Nice of you to grace us with your presence," Moose said as he moved past me to help Roach who was plating food at the stove.

"Kiss my ass, fucker. We got coffee?" I stepped up to where the pot sat and grabbed one of the cups already set out on the counter.

"Watch that language, Hawk, there's a lady present," Roach said, and all I could do was stare at him. When I glanced over at the table, Wild Bill, Keg, Crank, Tram, and Pinch shrugged, and Katie looked at me and smiled.

"Not sure even the coffee is going to help you. You look like shit, Hawk." With my free hand, I flipped Moose off and took the much needed first swig of hot brew.

I pulled the cup away from my mouth and said, "Not sleeping," then leaned my hip on the bar.

"Did something happen with the club while I was gone?" Wild Bill asked.

"Nah, pretty quiet actually." I took a swig of my coffee. Not sleeping was kicking my ass, and I knew who was to blame.

"Good. Glad to hear it. Maybe we are finally getting to some type of normalcy." Roach handed Wild Bill a plate of food.

"Like anything to do with this club is normal," Keg said, and we all agreed.

"Well, if it isn't Haven, then what's keeping you up at night?" Wild Bill asked as he started in on his food.

"Don't think it's a what, more a who. And she has red hair," Moose said as he sat a plate down in front of Katie and another on the table beside her where he sat down and joined her.

"Linc, stop it," Katie said as she picked up her fork and glared at Moose.

"Hey, when a phone call interferes with me getting laid, someone needs to answer for it. Ultimately, it was Hawk's fault for the call, which has now led to more calls," Moose said and shrugged.

"Oh my God, do you have bat hearing or what?" Katie swatted Moose's shoulder, and the others and I chuckled.

"I could be half deaf and still hear Charlie. I swear to God the woman only has one volume." Moose looked at me and continued, "Most of the time I can't make out what she's saying because the words run together 'cause she talks so damn fast, but every once in a while your name gets said. Brother, whatever happened between you two, it pissed her right the fuck off. I almost bet her ass isn't sleeping either."

"Does the club got a new hang-around?" Roach asked as he walked by with a plate in each hand and handed them off to Crank and Tram.

"No, she's not a hang-around." I finished off the first cup of coffee and poured another and joined everyone at the table.

"Sit down, Roach, and let their asses get their own food. What are you doing cooking anyway? You haven't been feeling well," Wild Bill said when Roach walked back and placed a plate in front of Keg.

"Oh hell, I had a touch of the flu, it's passed, and I besides, I ain't dead. Now, who is the new girl you're talking about?" Roach pulled out a chair and sat even though he bitched about it.

Pinch got up and grabbed his and Roach's plates and brought them back to the table. "Her name is Charlie Rhoades. She's a bounty hunter and rides a Harley. And woo wee, the woman is hot as fuck."

"Is she working around here?" Roach started to eat and asked Pinch.

"What the hell, Roach? I drop the f-bomb, and you jump my ass," I point between Moose and Pinch, "and those two say it and you don't even blink an eye."

"'Cause he likes us better than you, Hawk," Moose said and laughed.

Spencer "Roach" Danson was part of Haven before any of us at the table had joined. Wild Bill had offered him a leadership position in the club when he took over, but Roach had told him that he was too old for all that bullshit, and the youngsters should be brought up in the ranks. Roach wasn't that much younger than Shock and Freak. And like them, he had served in the military. When Haven decided to work on cleaning up the club most of the members were all for it. Not that any of us would say it out loud for fear of our throats being cut while we slept, but age was creeping up on a few of them and the possibility of getting caught running drugs and guns and spending their last years in jail was unappealing.

When I'd joined, Roach had been my sponsor, and I'd gotten to know him well over the years. He was a good man, but he didn't waste time on niceties, he said what was on his mind whether it pissed you off or not.

Roach finally answered me around the food in his mouth, "Those two," he pointed between Moose and Pinch, "and Keg are lost causes. I have more hope for you, Crank, and Tram." When Moose scowled at Roach, he only laughed. Katie joined him and earned her own glare from Moose.

"Don't give me that look, Linc. Roach has your number. Every other word out your mouth is a dirty word." Katie went back to eating.

"Oh, darlin', you don't seem to mind at night when I whisper dirty words in your ears." The blush on Katie's face came immediately. The others and I chuckled while Moose grinned.

Katie stood and picked up her empty plate. "Bunch of assholes," was heard as she walked around the table toward the sink. The chuckles turned into full-blown laughter. "If you are done embarrassing me, Linc, we should go. I don't want to be late."

"You working at the hospital today?" I sobered up and asked.

"No, I'm off today. This is my long weekend. My dad's hearing is today, and I want to be there." Katie reached for her purse that was on the bar, and Moose stood.

"Attorney got any idea on what the commission is going to smack him with?" Wild Bill asked. Moose moved beside Katie, and he was the one to answer.

"Paul won't be brokering anymore, that's for sure. The trade commission wanted the book thrown at him, but it helped that he finally came around and turned over everything financial he had on Kosnoff to the Feds. They're hoping to trace the money back to its origin to locate some of the young girls and women who were taken. That's going to be one tough fucking job, but if they find just one, it will be worth the time spent. Anyway, since Paul is cooperating, the attorney Alex set him up with is hopeful for probation,

41

especially if Mary's health issues are taken into account. We shall see. Never know what they'll do." Moose leaned down when he was finished and kissed the top of Katie's head.

"Let us know if you need us to help with anything. Church on Sunday to discuss next week. You can fill us in then on what happens today," Wild Bill said, and Moose nodded.

"That works. Katie and I will be here tomorrow night for the party. Be nice to see everyone in a relaxed atmosphere for a change. The men haven't had that for quite a while."

"I'll be here, too. We should all be there," I said.

"I won't be here. I'm going to test and rewire a couple of the devices you're going to need when you leave." Moose and I both frowned at Roach's words.

"Why are you doing Keg's job?"

"I'm right here, assholes. I won't be here either because I will be at Roach's place. Damn, give me more credit than that, brothers," Keg said, disgustedly. He was the one who took care of everything we used that had wiring or components in them. Roach had been teaching Keg everything he learned in the military.

"There are a few pieces he is having problems with and asked if I would take a look at them. Don't know how bad they are until we get inside them. I would have helped Keg earlier but being sick got me behind."

"Okay, was just making sure Keg wasn't shuffling his workload on you while he was getting his dick wet." I grinned when Keg flipped me off.

42

"We're out of here," Moose said and led Katie to the door, but before he could get her through it, she stopped and walked back to Roach and bent and kissed him on the cheek.

"Thanks, Spencer, for breakfast."

"Anytime, sweetheart," Roach said and smiled at her. I cocked my eyebrow in question at Moose, and he shrugged. Seemed all kinds of things were going on at the club. When I looked at Keg, Crank, Tram, and Pinch, they wore the same expression as me.

Moose and Katie said goodbye and walked out. I turned to Roach, who sat leisurely drinking his coffee. "What the hell is going on around here?" I asked, and Prez laughed. Hell, most of the time, we had to keep up with older members more than the prospects.

"What are you talking about?" Roach replied with his own question.

"You are surly on a good day. Now you are fixing breakfast for Moose's ol' lady." I didn't get to keep going with my rant.

"That girl brings life back into this club. She even came and checked on me at home," Roach said matter-of-fact like.

"First, Shock and Freak, now you." Everything I thought to say before left me. When I looked at Prez, he shrugged. Crank, on the other hand, didn't seem to suffer the same problem.

"We're going to turn into a club run by skirts." Crank shook his head.

43

"What are you bitching about, Crank?" Prez asked, but Crank didn't get to respond before Roach jumped in.

"You men are too young to understand it. We haven't had, but a few ol' ladies come through this club before Smoke's and Fire's ol' ladies, Tink and Macy. And those women are the best. They're tough and have last through the crap that Haven was plagued with, but they are only two people. Haven's turning over a new leaf, the club is strong again because of the new leadership, but that is not all that makes a club. The women who accept us, put up with our grouchy asses, and call us on our bullshit—they're what makes a club a family. Takes a lot to tear a strong family apart. If we'd had more women before, who knows, maybe the club wouldn't have suffered so much." Roach rose and poured himself another cup of coffee, then leaned on the counter. "Now who's going to fill me in on your redhead."

"She isn't my redhead." I threw my hands up in the air and Prez, Keg, Crank, Tram, and Pinch chuckled. They, in turn, got the double birds.

"Too bad, you don't know what you're missing. My Annie was a redhead. Kinda partial to them myself." Roach took a drink of his coffee, and I would've bet money on the brief look that crossed his face of one of regret.

"Yeah, I know what you mean, Roach. I for one, am glad Haven is moving forward. If anything, watching some of the changes happen has been enjoyable. And there will be more to come," Prez said, and we all agreed.

"Yeah, it is. Feels nice to be a part of something good again. Now...about the redhead?" Roach looked at me, and I

44

laughed. The man wasn't going to give it up. He'd been sick and missed some of what happened at the club.

"Charlie was Katie's neighbor over at the duplex. She moved here to take a job with the Matherson brothers. Don't know a whole lot about her other than she is a bounty hunter and moved here to look for her grandad." I shrugged.

"Oh, you boys helping her with that?" Roach asked and looked at each of us.

"No, hadn't thought about it. Don't even know any information on him. Didn't ask. Assumed the Matherson brothers are helping her out." I stood. "We going to go over the list, Prez?"

"Yeah, I saw it. Let's go to my office and knock that out. At least we can have one thing off our plates before you men take off on the job. Get through the basics of it and save the rest for Church," Prez said, stood and took his plate and cup to the sink. He and I nodded at the others and walked out.

After the nights of tossing and turning over Charlie and kicking myself for not just taking her up on her offer, I adjusted my pants as I sat down in a chair across from the prez. I needed to get Charlie out of my mind so I could focus on the upcoming job. I didn't need to be distracted. I could fuck her and get her out of my system, then move on. However, with her, I didn't think it would be that simple.

By the time Prez and I finished going over what would be needed for the job we had scheduled, the main room only had a few guys playing cards and a couple sitting with hang-arounds on their laps while they talked. I walked

45

up to the bar where Lora, one of the regular club girls, was leaning over talking to Crank. I smacked him on the back and took the seat next to him.

"Thought you were at Roadside working today?" I signaled for Lora to hand me a beer.

"Yeah, Pinch came in and took over the evening shift. Instead of staying at the bar, I stopped by here to have a beer before I headed home. Was going to check in with you and Prez when I was done to see if you need help with anything."

"Nah, we're good." I looked at Lora and jerked my head to the side. She knew the action meant to take a hike and walked out from behind the bar to join the others in the room. "Prez sent General Patel the list of weapons you requested. He emailed back that they will be in the motel rooms where we are staying. The complete file will be sent with any new intel they have. It should give us an idea of how big the threat is and what we might be facing when we get there."

"That's good. It'll allow us to make sure we have everything we need available."

"Yeah, worked out good."

"You headed home, too?" Crank asked.

"Might as well, this place is pretty quiet. Might stay here tomorrow night depending on how much I drink."

Crank's brows furrowed when he looked at me. "You okay, Hawk? Seem out of sorts lately. It's not like you, brother."

Geez, my brothers would have a field day riding my ass if they knew Charlie was keeping me from sleeping, which in turn, made my ass grouchy.

"Nothing that getting laid won't fix."

"I hear you."

I slapped Crank on the back and stood. "Going to get out of here. See you tomorrow, Crank."

"I might as well head out, too." Crank stood, and we walked out together. After we got on our bikes, we rode out together until I reached the turnoff for my place.

As I walked through the door my cell rang, and I answered the call from the contractor who was overseeing the renovations to the place I'd purchased a while back.

"Hey, Gary. What's up?" I listened to him while I walked through my place, grabbing a beer out of the fridge and sitting down at the table in the kitchen and pulling off my boots. "No shit," was out of mouth before what he said completely sank in.

"You heard me. Just those minor things I listed and it's ready for you to move in. Those will be done in the next couple day, so if you want to stop by tomorrow, I'll be there."

"Thanks, Gary. Man, you've done a great job for me. Won't forget it."

We talked a couple more minutes about all the work that had been done to the house before the call ended. Then I looked around the duplex as I made my way up the stairs to my bedroom, making a mental list of everything I needed to do.

The move to the house wasn't the only thing I needed to deal with either. Charlie. To pursue her or not. Why I was even debating it should have been a clue that it wasn't going to be as easy as I thought.

As I stretched out on my bed and closed my eyes, Charlie's face popped up, and yeah, nothing about her screamed easy.

CM Books, LLC

Chapter Three

Charlie

"Charlie? You still good?" Travis spoke through the earpiece.

"Why wouldn't I be good? I'm sitting in a tricked-out Pinto. In an alley. In a crappy neighborhood waiting to see if the asshole we've been hunting actually is visiting his seventy-year-old grandmother for her birthday. And I ran out of coffee two fucking hours ago. So yeah, everything is just peachy." Male laughter filled my ear.

"Tell us how you really feel, why don't ya," Jake said and continued to laugh.

"Hey, you guys asked. I don't know why we are all needed for this weasel. I read his record, and he is plain stupid. I mean, I understand why he jumped bail, the dumbass is on his third strike, but still, every time the cops were looking to arrest him, his grandmother's place is where they've picked him up. Umm...you'd think after the first time

49

he'd want to mix it up a bit. I don't know, have the grandmother meet him somewhere."

"What crawled up your ass today? You have been in a foul mood since you walked into the office this morning." Josh's voice sounded muffled.

"This morning? I thought it was part of her personality. She's been surly going on a week," Mitchell said.

"You're a dick, Mitchell. And, Josh, I know you are eating something." I hadn't gotten a chance to grab anything but coffee before the call came in on the guy we were searching for.

"Donuts. You should've grabbed some on the way here," Josh answered.

"Really? Travis said we needed to get here fast and you took the time to stop. What the hell?"

"Travis tends to be a little over the top," Mitchell said, then laughed.

"Fucktards, you know I can hear you, right?" I snorted at Travis's response. It was easy to forget the men were related most of the time. But then, out of nowhere they would say or do something that made me glad I was an only child.

"We got movement. Front curtain," Jake said, which stopped all talking.

The earbuds were silent as I watched the back of the building. Josh and Jake had the front while Travis sat at one end of the block and Mitchell at the other. Wyan Sampson was in his grandmother's apartment, I could feel it. And if the neighbor was right when she called the office, he'd been

50

there since four that morning. Thank God for Mrs. Johnson's insomnia. I could relate to what the woman suffered through. Except my sleeplessness had a different name, Kaden Cross. Hawk to his friends.

I felt the attraction to him the first time I met him. He acted interested, too, by the way he acted at the clubhouse the first time I was there. Then, when we cleared and cleaned up Katie's place, I saw how I affected him. Hell, he affected me with just his voice. I never had that happen with a man, ever. I liked going after whatever I wanted. Even prided myself on being bold and upfront. But with Kaden Cross, I found myself, for lack of a better term, wanting to be a girlie-girlie and let him take me to new heights. Something told me he could do it, too.

The fear of losing myself hadn't been strong enough to keep me away from him. The smart move would have been to stay as far away from him as possible, but I wasn't strong enough to do that. It had been over a week, and with each day I could feel myself caving.

Rejection never bothered me before. Some men couldn't deal with an aggressive woman, I totally got that. With Kaden, his dismissal had hurt, especially when I saw the desire in his eyes, and my first response was to get angry and go on the defensive.

After long and sexually frustrated nights, the only resolve I managed was I wouldn't let him get to me. He didn't want what I had to offer, fine. It would be a cold day in hell when I offered again. Yeah, that sounded like a lie even to me.

"Charlie? Charlie!" Travis's voice pulled me back to what I was there for in the first place.

"Dude, do you need to yell?" I said while I stuck my finger in my ear and shifted the earbud around.

"When you don't answer. Yes. I've been talking for two minutes. Did you catch any of it?"

Like I would admit I zoned out thinking about a man. "The earbud must have a short or something. It was silent until you yelled my name a dozen times. What did I miss?" The others chuckled but didn't say a word.

"The equipment is tested regularly, but whatever. We don't have time to get to the bottom of why you weren't answering. Any movement in the window you've got eyes on?"

"No. I would have said something. I know the procedure. I'm not a damn rookie at this, Travis."

"Didn't you just say the earbud wasn't working?" More laughter followed Travis's response.

"Didn't you just say we didn't have time for this? What did you need to tell me?" Seemed like assholishness was making it through all the males I knew.

"Fine, we'll discuss your lack of response later." Travis's no-nonsense voice pierced my ear.

"Can't wait," I muttered.

"If Wyan heads out the back and makes you, don't engage him by yourself. We got the ends of the block covered; he won't get away." I tried not to lose my temper; it was the first case we all worked on together. I had only started at their company, but they had witnessed my work

52

when we were after the same fugitive before. The brothers held licenses in several states and were called upon for special fugitive recovery due to their skip tracing ability.

I crossed paths with Jake and Josh in Maryland where I worked for a bail bond agency that was run by one of my dad's retired Air Force buddies.

"Is there a reason you doubt my ability today, or is this going to be a reoccurring thing I have to deal with? I'm not going to have you hamp—" Travis cut me off.

"Fuck, don't get your panties in a wad. If you read Wyan's file, then you know he may be a little on the slow side, mentally, but the man is huge. I'm just saying, I know you have your vest on, but that doesn't mean he won't try to take you out. He's desperate, Charlie. And desperate people do dumb shit. I don't want to see you hurt if it could've been avoided in the first place. So wait for backup. That's all I was saying." I heard the sigh as Travis finished. And I couldn't argue with the logic behind it.

"Fine, but if he jets, I can't promise I won't try to slow him down." I heard the groans from the brothers and continued, "Trust me. I'm not going to do anything stupid. I told you I read the man's file. He's six foot eight, and he has two hundred seventy pounds on me at his three ninety. Not including the damn near foot and a half or more in height difference. So what? Did you expect me to tackle the man? Why? When I carry the Tase C2 or the X2 Defender. My toys never let me down."

"Yeah, yeah. You're like a little ninja," Mitchell said, and the others laughed.

53

"Got movement!" Josh yelled over the laughter, and everyone stopped laughing, and from Josh's voice I heard, "Fuck, he spotted us."

"Son-of-a-bitch, he's cutting between the buildings," Jake said, and I heard vehicle doors slam and knew they were on the chase.

"Charlie, he is going to come out the opposite side of the building you are watching," Josh huffed.

"Mitchell and I are on the move," Travis said, and I could hear engines start in the background. They would each enter the alley from the two ends and corner Wyan, leaving him nowhere to go.

Well, that was if everything worked out.

I hit the corner of the building just as the fugitive barreled out into the alley and before I could raise the taser, he hit me full force. I closed my eyes, and the only thing I thought was when I hit the ground it was going to hurt like a motherfucker, because not only was I falling, but so was the big ass fugitive who had grabbed ahold of me when we ran into each other.

On the way down, the big man turned us and hit the pavement with me on top of him. I expected to hear the thud as his head hit the ground, but it didn't happen. Nope, however, the pain that shot through my face had me gritting my teeth and squeezing my eyes shut tighter.

"What the fuck, Wyan?" I heard Travis yell as hands grabbed my arms and lifted me until I was on my feet.

54

"Charlie, are you okay?" I opened my eyes to see Travis bent down eye level with me. I raised my hand to my face and felt around until I found the area that hurt.

"Fuck that hurts. Is it bleeding?" I asked and moved my hand away to look at it. Thank God, there was no blood.

"No, but you are going to have one helluva shiner," Mitchell said as he rolled Wyan over and Josh cuffed him.

It took the three men to help lift the fugitive to his feet, and I might've laughed if I was concentrating on not passing out from the pain.

"Christ, did he get a punch in on the way down or what?" I continued to touch the spot right below my left eye to check if my cheekbone was cracked or broken.

"Not a punch, it was his forehead that made contact with your face. When you two hit the ground, it jarred his head forward," Travis said and moved my hand to take a closer look. "You are going to the hospital and have that checked out."

"I don't feel anything broken. I'll put some ice on it and go by Katie's house and have her take a look." I hated hospitals and avoided them at all cost.

"Goddamn, you are hardheaded. You could have a damn concussion, but I'm not going to stand here and argue with you. We need to take Wyan in and turned him over." Travis turned to the big man and said, "Why the fuck did you run when you saw us, Wyan? You knew you didn't have anywhere to go."

"Come on, Trav. I can't go to jail, man. Those cells aren't big enough. I'll go crazy in there." I looked between the two men.

"And I put money up so you could stay out of them until your court date. Which you wouldn't have had a court date if you hadn't sold that bag to the undercover officer." Travis moved closer to Wyan and stood in front of him and lowered his voice. "I know you want to help out your grandmother. But, Wyan, didn't I tell you to stay away from the Widows? That they are only using you? We're not going to be able to help you if you keep getting in trouble. It's your third strike, I'm not sure we're going to be able to keep you out."

"Am I missing something here? Do you know Pillsbury?" I asked Travis as I stepped closer to where I still stood to the side but between Travis and the apprehended fugitive, then pointed with my thumb to the big guy.

"Pillsbury?" Mitchell asked.

"Yeah, you know, 'cause when we fell, he cushioned the fall. Like the doughboy." I waved my hand as if they should know what I was talking about and continued to look at Travis. "So?"

"You got a fairy working for ya, Trav?" Wyan said, and the others snorted.

"Seriously? You are standing there cuffed, on your way to jail, and you feel the need to crack a joke." I looked up at the big man.

"You tried it," he said and smiled down at me. The expression changed his whole face. The man looked like a giant teddy bear. I couldn't help myself, I smiled back, which instantly reminded me that my face hurt.

"Tried? Mine was funny," I said.

Wyan's response of, "Not really," had the guys snickering.

"Oh, a comedian that takes down women on his off time. You're a riot, dude," I said sarcastically.

"Can we get back to what we are here for?" Travis got everyone's attention.

"I like her, Trav."

"Glad you approve. Wyan, we've got to turn you in, but I will see what we can come up with to help you. I can't promise anything, man. You messed up. I know you've been trying to help your grandmother out, but you need to find a different way. Who's going to look out for her while you are locked up? The Widows won't."

Wyan's face fell, and he nodded. Sometimes doing the right thing sucked. Wyan had to be taken in, or the Matherson Bail Bond Agency would be out the cash they put up for Wyan's bail, but I didn't have to like it. I found myself feeling sad for the man. If he had wanted to hurt me, he only had to fall on me instead of turning us at the last minute.

"Appreciate you not flattening me on the pavement, dude. That would have hurt a lot more than this," I said and touched my cheek.

"No one should hurt girls," Wyan said and smiled.

"Come on, Wyan, you can ride with me," Mitchell said and grabbed the big man's elbow.

57

"I'll meet you there," Travis said as Mitchell lead Wyan to his vehicle. No one said anything until the two were pulling away.

"Gonna tell me what the deal is with him?" I asked, and Josh was the one who answered.

"We went to school with Wyan. He was a grade ahead of us. He struggled through school because of his learning disability. Kids were cruel, and they would make friends with him just so they could make fun of him. They thought because he was slow, he didn't understand what they were doing. Wyan has always been big, even in grade school and by high school, he towered over everyone."

"Umm...you guys aren't exactly small," I interrupted.

"No, but we didn't sprout until we were in high school. But what Josh is trying to tell you in his roundabout way." Josh flipped Travis off, but he ignored him and continued, "We friended him and started watching out for him. Some of the jocks in the school lost their means of entertainment and didn't appreciate it, so they decided we were the reason. One day six of them caught Mitchell out after he had dropped his girlfriend off. They jumped him, and Mitchell was holding his own the best he could with the odds. About five minutes into the fight, Wyan happened to walk up and saw Mitchell getting a beating and stepped in. He pulled the boys off Mitchell and beat the living shit out of them. So, we have a history with him. We do what we can for him. Now let's get going. Josh and Jake, you go back to the office and, Charlie, you head out for the day and get that eye looked at."

"I'll go back to the office and put some ice on it while I help Josh and Jake fill out the paperwork. I can have Katie look at the eye at the party tonight. You guys still going, right?"

"Yeah, we planned to, so we can go together, and if Katie thinks you need to go have that x-rayed, then your ass is going to do just that," Travis said and glared at me.

"Fine. I'm surrounded by men with the need to boss me around. Did I tell you I don't do well that?" Travis grunted and started walking off.

"I'm going with he doesn't give a shit," Josh said as we watched Travis get in his truck and pull away.

"Meet you back at the office. And just so you know, I'm stopping at Taco Bell and not bringing you shit." I turned and started toward the car.

"Hey, I want tacos! I didn't get to eat any of the donuts," Jake yelled as I opened the car door and got in.

When I pulled out, I rolled the window down, and as I passed by the twins, I yelled, "Sucks to be you!"

Then I couldn't help but laugh when they both pouted and yelled back, "But we're hungry, too," in little boy voices.

When I'd taken the job offer from the brothers, they'd come across as complete alphas, since working with them, I'd gotten to witness a softer side of them.

After I pulled in the lot behind the office building and shut the car off, I looked in the mirror at my face for the first time. I was definitely going to have a shiner. The eye was already swelling, and the cheekbone area was puffy, red, and the bruising had begun. Yeah, Katie needed to take a look at it.

As I walked in the back door with enough tacos to feed ten people, one thing crossed my mind—sure hoped today wasn't a prelude to how it was going to be working here. On the other hand, at least it wouldn't be boring.

CM Books, LLC

Chapter Four

Hawk

"That is great about the house. When are you going to try to move in?" Wild Bill asked as he and I sat down at the bar.

"Depending on when we have to fly out for the job. Either before I leave or after. No hurry. House isn't going anywhere. Plus the place I'm renting, they knew I would leave as soon as the house was done, so it won't be a big deal there," I said and turned around on the stool to face the room just as Ginger walked in adjusting her short skirt with Latch following behind her.

"Good to see the men with smiles on their faces and enjoying themselves." Wild Bill looked around the room.

"Prez, you're not that old to remember a woman can make the worst day seem brighter." When I looked over at Prez, he was smiling.

"No, I had one that made every day I woke up with her better than the day before. I'm not opposed to finding that again. Just don't think I'm going to find it with one of the club girls."

"Not working out with the woman you're seeing?"

Wild Bill's eyebrows shot up. "How the hell do you know I'm seeing anyone?" he questioned, and I smirked.

"What can I say. I'm the VP. You know, like you, Prez, my job is to know what's going on in the club. Besides, you know how I live to piece together intel."

"Yeah, yeah. Who knows?"

"When the prez leaves on a Saturday evening, twice a month, and comes back Sunday afternoon like clockwork...the VP and Sergeant of Arms investigates."

"Bullshit, how the hell did you two find out?"

"You wound me. I specialized in intelligence." I placed my hand over my heart for emphasis, and Wild Bill laughed and shook his head.

"Did you assholes follow me?"

"Nah, Taylor and Latch never miss being here on Saturday nights. But for two Saturdays a month, one shows, the other doesn't. On that Saturday, you don't stay long. It's been going on for the last eleven months by what we can tell. Prez, Moose and I are just happy you take someone with you."

"I'm going to head out after the others show tonight," Prez said, then looked over my shoulder and spoke, "How's it going, Latch."

"Prez, VP," Latch said and walked around the bar and grabbed a beer. "Get you another?" he asked and Prez and I both declined.

When the door opened, I looked up and watched Travis Matherson and his brothers walk in. I hadn't noticed Charlie until the brothers separated and she stepped between them, then looked around the room.

"Holy hell," Prez said at the same time I was up off the stool once we got a glimpse of her face.

I reached her, cupped her face in my hands, and tilted her head up so I could get a good look at it. She grabbed my wrists as if to stop me.

"What the hell are you doing? Let go of my damn face. The son-of-a-bitch hurts." At her words, I dropped my hands.

"Who the fuck punched her? I want a name, right…fuckin'…now." I glared at Travis.

"Nobody fuckin' punched her. Do you really think we would have let that happen? You need to step back, Hawk."

"You're at Haven, Travis. You might want to do the stepping back. I should kick your ass for even letting her get hurt, regardless of how it happened." I knew I was being slightly irrational, but when I saw that she was hurt, there was no way to contain the need to protect her.

"Oh hell, you're the reason she's been bitchy," Josh said, and when I turned to him and glared, he threw his hands up. "Whoa, we didn't show up to cause trouble. We showed up for some lovin'."

"For the love of God, Josh, shut up," Mitchell said and popped the back of Josh's head. Jake, Josh's twin, turned on Mitchell and Travis turned on all his brothers.

"Fuck, can we not go anywhere that you guys don't start acting like you're goddamn five. Christ, Mom should've have listened to me and smothered the three of you years ago. My life would be so much quieter."

"Bro, you would have been so lonely." Josh laughed.

"I'd be willing to chance that," Travis said and turned back to me. "Charlie had a little run-in with a guy we were chasing. She wouldn't go to the hospital and let them look at it. Said she'd have Katie do it when we came here."

"Hello, I am right the fuck here. And the last time I looked in the mirror, a grown ass woman looked back at me. So guess what, assholes? I can answer for myself." When I looked down at Charlie, she had her arms crossed over her chest, and her chin stuck out.

"That so?" I asked, and she nodded. "Know what I see when I look in the mirror?"

"A dick." At her response, Travis and his brothers and even Wild Bill snickered.

"Don't be a smartass. I see someone a whole lot bigger than you. Which means your ass is going to the hospital to get checked out. Let's go." I grabbed her arm and went to turn her toward the door when she jerked her arm out of my grip.

"Stop manhandling me, Kaden, or you're going to be embarrassed when I kick your ass in front of your club. Now get over yourself."

"The only person going to be embarrassed is you, when I turn you over my knee and spank your ass red." I turned to Prez, "Anyone bring their cage tonight that we can borrow? I will force her ass into it, and you can drive." I had no clue why the man beside grinned, and when he didn't answer, I looked down at Charlie.

"Well, you rode here so I guess you can ride on the back of my bike to the hospital. Now move it." I gestured to the door.

"I'm not going to the hospital. I'm meeting Katie here, dumbass. When I called her, she and Moose were headed here. Not like I owe you a fucking explanation. Nor did I come to this party to see you. So why don't you go find yourself a fake Barbie and leave me alone? I'll wait for Katie outside."

Charlie turned toward the door. Instead of arguing with her, I just bent and picked her up and started toward the kitchen. "You got one smart mouth, but I know what would keep that mouth occupied. Keep it up."

"Put me down, asshole!" Charlie kicked her leg back, and I slid one arm down to hold her against my body to save my nuts. My other arm was wrapped around her chest as I held her back to me. I lifted her enough so she couldn't swing her head back and bust me in the face. I had no doubt she'd do both if given the opportunity.

Travis and his brothers stepped toward me, and I saw Wild Bill step in front of them and shake his head. Then he said something I couldn't hear. Whatever it was stopped the men from following us.

"What're you doing, Hawk?" Moose asked as he and Katie walked in before I made it out of the room.

"Katie can look at Charlie in the kitchen." I walked to the kitchen and didn't realize Prez had followed us until a chair was pulled out.

"Thanks." I released the hold on Charlie and let her slide down my body until she stood on her feet.

"I should knock the crap out of you. The nerve. Like you have any right in what I do."

"Sit."

Charlie didn't move. Instead, her eyes hit me, and she sneered. "You can't boss me." She crossed her arms over her chest and glared up at me. Her one eye was damn near swelled shut, and there was purple bruising across her cheekbone. It had to hurt, and more than what she mentioned when I grabbed her earlier.

"Helluva shiner you got working there, Charlie. Hope the other guy looks worse," Moose said as he and Katie entered the room behind us.

"It's not a big deal. Shit happens. Part of the job," Charlie's words pissed me off.

"Sit your ass in that damn chair and let Katie take a look."

Charlie plopped in the chair with a huff but with no argument, which told me it had to hurt more than she was letting on.

I turned to see what was taking so long and the others stood to the side staring at us. Katie, with her mouth hanging open, and Prez, Moose, and Crank, who at some point had entered the room, with smirks on their faces. Dicks. Katie finally moved toward Charlie, sitting a bag on the table. When she opened it, I noticed it held medical supplies.

"Could she have broken the cheekbone?" I asked and leaned over to get a better look.

"Hawk, can you move, so I do my job?" Katie asked, and I looked at her. She smiled at me and pointed to Charlie. "I might be able to tell, and I need to make sure the eye isn't damaged, but you are blocking my view."

Crank and Moose chuckled. I flipped them off, stepped back, and crossed my arms over my chest. Charlie and I were going to have to come to terms with a few things. The first one would be about avoiding each other. That crap was over. She'd and I both would have to get used to it.

CM Books, LLC

Chapter Five

Charlie

"Shit, that freakin' hurts." I closed my eyes and took a deep breath while Katie poked around my cheekbone.

"Sorry, Charlie," Katie said, then continued, "I have to push so I can feel the bone. And even then, it could be fractured, and I wouldn't be able to feel that. You need an x-ray to tell for sure."

"Does she need to go have one done?" Kaden asked, and Katie's lips twitched when I rolled my eyes.

"I don't think it is necessary, Kaden. I didn't feel any lose bone fragments moving around, so that's a good sign. She doesn't look to have a concussion, but by the color of the bruising it is understa—"

"Excuse me," I pointed to myself, "I'm right here. Why are you talking to him?"

"Sorry—"

"Don't say it." Katie bit her lip, and I knew it was to keep from laughing. "Some bedside manner you have. And you," I pointed at Kaden. "Why are you standing over me as if I'm a prisoner who needs to be guarded?"

Before Kaden could answer, the door that led to the basement swung open, and Steven and Frankie stepped into the kitchen.

"We thought we heard you two up here," Frankie said as he looked between Katie and I. When his eyes stopped on me, his brows furrowed. "Who the fucking hell punched you?" At Frankie's question, Steven stepped around him to get a better look.

"Damn, who did that shit to you?" Steven said, and then he looked at the men in the room. "Hope like hell you boys put a beating on the bastard."

"Nobody punched me, guys. It happened on the job. The man we were apprehending, his forehead caught me in the face when he and I were falling to the ground." The whole room went quiet, but it only lasted five seconds.

"You goddamned tackled a grown ass man. What the hell is wrong with you? Better yet, what the hell is wrong with Travis and the others to put you in that position?" Kaden's voice rose with each word. "I should have kicked their asses earlier."

"I didn't tackle him!" I yelled to stop Kaden's tirade. "And why are you yelling? I don't know if I have a headache from the accident or from all the testosterone in this room. There is enough in the air that I'm pretty sure Katie and I could sprout chest hair just from absorbing it into our bodies."

70

Katie snickered, and the other men chuckled except for Kaden. His lips twitched, and he glanced down to my chest, then back to make eye contact with me.

"If you want, I can check to make sure that's not happening." I glared at Kaden as he smirked.

"You're a jerk." I had no clue why the hell he was so mad before. Now a smartass remark. As if his rejection of me at his place wasn't enough, now he wanted to be a dick on top of it. Plain bullshit.

Katie cleared her throat and broke eye contact with Kaden and looked at her. "I'll give you a script for pain pills. Get it filled. The pain will more than likely get worse before it starts to feel better, and there is no sense in you suffering through it. You also need to ice the area for no more than ten minutes at a time. Keep that up until you notice the swelling coming down. A good judge for that will be when the eye starts to open more. If you keep icing it down, I don't think it will swell completely shut." Katie pulled a tablet and pen out of the bag. Once she had the prescription filled out, she went to hand it to me, but before I could reach for it, Kaden grabbed it.

"Katie, doesn't she need someone to watch her?" Steven asked.

"Yes," Katie said and then turned to me. "I was going to suggest that you come to the house and stay with Moose and me."

"I am not going to impose on you two. I will be fine."

"That is what friends do for each other. Those pain pills are going to do a number on you. I would feel better if you stayed so I could keep an eye on you."

"She can stay here, and Shock and I will keep an eye on her." All I could do was look at Frankie when he spoke using Steven's club name. The room went silent until finally Crank, who I had forgotten was still there, broke it.

"As amusing as all this is, I'm going back to the main room and have a beer. Prez, brothers, ladies," Crank said and headed toward the door.

"If I'm not needed, I think I'm going to head out. Charlie, let Katie fix you up. And if you need to have someone around, you are more than welcome to use one of the rooms here." Wild Bill turned to Frankie and Steven. "If she stays, I'm leaving you two in charge of her." The men nodded at Wild Bill.

Everyone at Haven MC had been friendly to me from the first time I walked into the club. It meant a lot to me that they accepted me into the mix without a second thought. I knew it wasn't something that happened often. The small changes in Frankie and Steven since the first time I met them hadn't gone unnoticed either. Even though I had no intention of staying, the gesture from the men was nonetheless sweet.

"Don't worry about Charlie, I got her," Kaden said and then placed his hand on my shoulder. I'm surprised I didn't add whiplash to my injury when I jerked my head and looked up at him. I opened my mouth to speak, but before I could say anything, he continued, "Not going to listen to you argue about it. I will follow you home, and on the way we'll stop and get the prescription filled." I felt a light squeeze on my shoulder.

Katie, all of a sudden was busy closing up her bag, and Moose stood by her ready to pick it up. "Since you got it covered, Hawk, we are going in to join the others." A look passed between the two men, and each nodded to the other.

"Linc, I'm not sur—" Katie started but didn't get what she was going to say out before she was cut off by Moose.

"Hawk's handling it, Katie." Katie stared at Linc, and he stared back. Then she closed her bag, picked it up, and smacked it into his chest. All the while everyone in the room watched them. Frankie and Steven chuckled and Kaden, well instead of his hand on my shoulder, he moved it and started softly running his hand from the top of my head and down the back of my hair, then he would start over. I had every intention to stop him, but his touch felt nice. The gesture actually eased my headache. I was going to have to dig deep for the mad I had toward him earlier. The tender side of him could be my downfall.

"Fine," was said to Moose, then Katie walked over and bent to hug me. In my ear, she whispered, "Call if you need me."

"Going to head back downstairs since everything is handled. We might come back up in a bit." Frankie turned toward the door leading downstairs with Steven behind him.

"What do you mean back up in a bit, brother?" Moose asked, and Steven was the one to answer.

CM Books, LLC

"The party, Moose. We haven't decided if we want to join it," Steven said over his shoulder as he and Frankie went through the doorway and pulled the door closed behind them.

For the first time since I arrived at Haven, I wanted to laugh but refrained myself by biting my lip. I looked at Katie, and she was doing the same. Wild Bill, Moose, and Kaden however, stared at the closed door. Wild Bill recovered first.

"Do you think they plan to actually come to the party?"

I lost the little composure I held at that moment, and Katie joined me as we laughed.

"Why are you laughing?" Kaden asked.

"You men look so out of sort all because they," I motioned with my arm to the door the men went through, "mentioned attending the party. What is up with that?"

"You know some of their issues?" I nodded, and Kaden continued, "Freak and Shock don't do well with the noise and so many people moving around. They normally stay downstairs away from it. So them mentioning about joining in, is huge where they are concerned. Now come on, let's get you up and home." Kaden grabbed my arm to help me up. When I stood, he let go of my arm and placed his hand in the middle of my back.

"They probably don't plan to stay, maybe just come up and say hey. I wouldn't read too much into it." Moose put his arm around Katie and started to lead her out the door with Wild Bill behind them. Kaden nudged me in the same direction. I looked up at him over my shoulder.

74

"Stop being pushy. You don't need to follow me home either. I'm perfectly capable of getting to my house on my own. You wouldn't want to miss the party. I'm sure the women would be disappointed."

"Uh huh," was his reply as he continued to lead me out behind the others.

"I mean it. I don't need a babysitter."

"Be quiet and keep moving, Red. Don't make me put you over my shoulder and carry your ass out."

"Don't call me that. You're a bossy bastard, and if you think you are going to tell me what to—" Kaden moved in front of me and stopped our progress of leaving. He then bent his head until his mouth was by my ear.

"Don't try me. You're in pain, I can see it even though you're trying to hide it. You can bust my balls later, just let me help you now, Red." Kaden's warm breath brushed over my ear as he whispered in it and I lost what little fight I had in me. He was right, I was in enough pain that I couldn't think, but I had no plans to share that with him.

"I don't like being called that."

"You'll get used to it."

"Whatever, you can follow me, and we can stop at the drugstore on the way if it makes you feel better. I promise to be a good little girl and take my medication and stay in my house." Kaden stepped back and motioned me forward again.

We reached the spot where Travis, Mitchell, Jake, Josh, and I had parked our bikes. Kaden walked to the bike on the other side of mine, which goes to show how much pain I was in when I arrived at Haven that I hadn't even noticed Kaden's bike. Wild Bill came around the building on his bike and waved at us on his way out of the lot with another bike following behind him. I straddled my bike and started it, then looked over at Kaden.

"Go slow, and I'll be right behind you!" Kaden yelled over the rumbling of my pipes and started his bike, then motioned with his head for me to pull out first. I had a brief thought about how it would feel to leave him behind, and I might have done it if I was at a hundred percent. Instead, I did the smart and safe thing.

The pharmacy at the local drugstore wasn't busy, and I handed over my prescription and insurance card. While I stepped off to the side to wait for it to be filled, Kaden walked off. When he returned, he had a carry-all in his hand with several items inside. I watched him from my spot as he stopped at the shelves located in front of the pharmacy area and began looking over the items there. I walked over and stood beside him.

"Really?" was the only response I could get out, and he looked at me over his shoulder as he squatted down and reached for an item.

"What?" He stood back up and placed the item in his carry-all.

"I'm adding arrogant to your list," I said, then started toward the counter as I heard my name called. Kaden was on my heels.

"Not seeing what has you riled now." He honest to God had no clue as he looked down in the carry-all, which

76

had me looking down into it, too. There was shampoo, deodorant, a package of razors, a toothbrush, and his new addition.

"The condoms!" The girl at the counter bowed her head, but I didn't miss the smile on her face as she rang up my sale. "I hope you don't think you will be using those tonight. And please don't be embarrassed to buy the correct size in front of me. I promise I won't judge." I stepped to the side so he could place his things on the counter for the girl to ring up.

"Damn, Red, did you think they were for you? I'm not a desperate man who would have to fuck someone in pain just to get off. I'm low on them just like the other items. We are here, I thought I would grab a few things and save me an extra trip. No ulterior motive involved. As for the size..." he paused and winked at the salesgirl, who giggled, then he continued, "Trojan Magnum XL Lubricated is the only ones I've found to fit me decent enough to get the job done. The lubrication is so the woman and I both get to enjoy the experience. It's as hard on a man, no pun intended, to fight to get inside as it is on the woman, so it makes the slide in a lot easier for both of us. I'm a big man, Red." Kaden paid for his purchase and turned with his bag. "All over."

Kaden didn't wait for me to reply before he started for the front of the store. I looked at the salesgirl and told her thank you as she handed me the prescription. She smiled at me and then leaned across the counter and lowered her voice.

77

"You are one lucky lady. That man defines the phrase 'sex on a stick.'" I nodded and walked off to catch up, there was nothing to respond back with. As I got closer to Kaden and followed him, I took inventory. He was tall, and from his sandy blond hair to his big broad shoulders to the narrow waist that led down to thick thighs that pulled the jean material tight, his body formed the perfect V. And his ass filled the jeans out to the point it made me wonder if I could bounce a quarter on it.

"Red," was said and fingers were snapped in front of my face.

"What?"

"I said your name like three times. Come on, we don't have far to go. Let's get you home, dosed up, and in bed," he said and smirked.

I got busted staring, but suddenly I didn't have enough energy to care. The adrenaline from the day and everything else combined with it was wearing off quickly. I wanted my home, my bed, and maybe a dozen hours of sleep. With that in my mind, I slipped the store bag into my saddlebag and mounted my bike. After Kaden did the same, we were on our way.

Chapter Six

Hawk

Charlie was so done by the time we got to her place that she hadn't even questioned when I pulled my bike in the garage with hers. I got her in the house, up the stairs to her room, and I grab her pills and a baggie of ice while she changed into an oversized t-shirt.

"Thanks." She got in bed, and I handed her the pills and a bottle of water I had grabbed from her fridge. "Can you make sure the garage door closes when you leave. Don't worry about arming the security system, it will be fine for tonight."

After she'd swallowed the pills and laid down, I placed the ice bag on her cheek. "Won't need to, I'm staying."

"You don't need to stay. I'll be fine," Charlie said and yawned hugely.

"Not going to leave you by yourself. Don't forget what Katie said about those pills. Staying, so not in the mood to argue."

79

"Okay, fine. Do what you want. There are blankets and an extra pillow in the hall closet for the couch. I don't have a bed in the extra bedroom. I have that set up as an office." When her eyes closed, I knew the pills were kicking in. I sat on the side of the bed and waited so I could remove the bag of ice when the ten minutes were up.

I leaned over her and inspected her eye and cheek. "At least the swelling looks to have stopped, that's a good sign. The purple bruising, though, has started to turn black."

"Uh huh," Charlie mumbled and then sighed. I couldn't help myself, I reached out and moved the hair from around her face and then ran my knuckles softly down the side, careful not to brush her injury.

"What is it about you, Red? You're different from every woman I've been around. One minute you piss me off, the next I want to take you to bed and not let you up," I spoke softly not to disturb her and eased off the bed removing the ice bag. I tossed it in the sink in the bathroom and walked to the other side of the bed and stripped. Once I was in bed, I leaned over her and turned the lamp off, then settled back onto the pillow.

"My winning personality," was whispered into the darkness, and I chuckled and unable to stop myself, I pulled Charlie into my arms. I waited for her to protest. Instead, she snuggled into my side and laid her head on my chest, and it didn't escape me that she fit as if she belonged there. Even more, was the fact it didn't bother me that she did.

"Yeah, Red, that's gotta be it." I turned and kissed her head, then smiled and closed my eyes.

80

I noticed a few things as I started to wake, it wasn't daylight yet, and warm breath was touching my chest. I opened my eyes, and a pair of green ones looked back at me.

"You know, you are one of the best looking men I've seen." Charlie smiled and continued to look me in the eyes. The swelling was down, but the bruising was black across her cheek and circling her eye, but even with that, she was beautiful.

"How many of those pain pills did you take this morning?"

She smacked my chest and leaned up on her elbow. "None. It hurts but surprisingly not like it did yesterday. I'll switch to Tylenol or Motrin instead of that stuff Katie prescribed. Shit knocked me right out." Charlie's leg that rested on mine moved up and down. "Now, want to tell me why you are in my bed?"

I put the arm that wasn't wrapped around her behind my head and looked down at her. "You needed to be watched. Couldn't do that from the couch and I sure as hell wasn't bunking on the floor."

Charlie raised up, threw her leg over me, then shifted her body until she straddled my waist, her chin rested on her hands on my chest. I moved my freed arm and crossed it with the one I already had behind my head.

"So, why Hawk as a club name?"

"It started with my stint in the military. I was tagged with it because there isn't much I miss. I can be in a place with a hundred people around, and I will find the one person who doesn't belong. When I prospected with Haven, they continued to call me it after they saw the tat on my back."

She pushed up and sat with her knees rested at my sides. Charlie rubbed my chest with her hands and grazed her nails lightly over my nipples, causing them to pebble from the attention as I watched her explore my body.

"Not many tats on the front of you, though. I guess the flag with the weapons crossed over it represents the military." She touched the upper part of my arm and outlined the tattoo. Then she moved her other hand to my other arm and did the same to the tat there. "This one is for Haven." Charlie ran both her hands back until they were on my chest rubbing it once again. "And nothing marring this beautiful chest." She wiggled, and the material of her shirt moved revealing she didn't have any panties on as I felt her pussy touch the skin on my stomach. Touching me was making her wet by the moisture I felt as she slid her hips forward and then back.

Shit, the woman was killing me. "No panties, Red?"

She went to slide back, which would have put her on my cock, but I wasn't ready for her to be there, so I moved my arms from behind my head and grabbed hold of her thighs to still her movement.

"I don't sleep in them." She leaned forward and ran her tongue around one of my nipples, then licked across my chest to do the same to the other one. My cock twitched and moved against my thigh. It had gone hard the minute Charlie began to explore me with her hands. The only thing that kept it from tenting the sheet was its weight.

"What are you up to, Red?" I asked as she stretched her body and licked up my chest to reach my neck. I moved my hands from her thighs and cupped her ass. She was small compared to me; the globes of her ass fit into my hands perfectly. I squeezed them, and she took it as a 'continue on' and moved her tongue up my neck, reaching my chin where she stopped to nibble.

"I'm going to show you what you passed on before," Charlie said and sucked on my chin. My dick jumped with just the thought of that mouth wrapped around it.

"I didn't take a pass because I didn't want what you offered. It had more to do with taking control of the situation."

"You're letting me be in control now." She slid up until her face was looking down on mine, leaving a trail of moisture on my skin from her journey.

"Letting is the keyword." I ran one of my hands up her back and tangled it into the wild red mass. Charlie had thick, uncontrollable hair that seemed to fit who she was. I used the grip I had on her hair to bring her face closer to mine. "And your time is up." I slammed our lips together, and when she gasped, I dove in with my tongue. It only took a second for the shock of the move to wear off and Charlie to become invested in the kiss as much as I was. Her lips were soft to my hard, but it didn't stop me from brutalizing them with my teeth and tongue. She moaned around my tongue, and the sound wasn't related to passion, I pulled back. "Fuck, Red. I forgot about your face. Did I hurt you, baby?"

"No, yes. It hurts a little when the skin gets touched on that side. Your nose brushed the area."

Christ, I felt like the asshole she accused me of being. "Aww, Red, I'm sorry." I cupped her face between my hands and pulled her back down and kissed the area gently with my lips.

"It's okay, Kaden. I'm not going to break." She raised up and looked at me.

"You're not, huh?"

"Nope."

"Come here," I said and moved my hands under her arms and started pulling her up.

"What are you doing?"

"Going to make you forget about the pain."

I continued to pull her up until she sat on my chest. My hands went to her thighs and lifted her toward my face. "Place those knees on each side of my head, Red, and grab hold of that headboard, you're going to need the support."

Charlie grabbed the headboard like I told her, and as she moved into position, I saw the signs of her desire with her glistening pussy poised above me. She wasn't shaved bare, the hair left was a strip down the middle, and it was groomed close. The scent of her desire had my tongue darting out and sliding through her folds, and the shiver that went through her body showed she liked what I was doing to her.

"Get a good grip on the headboard, Red. I'm going to give you the control you like." I moved my hands to the front and used my thumbs to spread her wide, then sucked

84

her clit into my mouth, using my tongue to press against the swollen bud. Then I released her from my mouth. "Ride my tongue, baby." I pierced her opening with my tongue, and her hips jerked. It didn't take her long to find a rhythm that worked for her, my tongue hitting her clit on every pass.

Charlie's legs started to quiver, and I knew she was close and took over. Grabbing her thighs, I held her still while I sucked, nipped, and licked. When she threw her head back, I licked her slit and used my thumb and finger from one hand to pinch the sensitive nub, which caused her orgasm to roll through her, and she exploded onto my tongue. I licked and sucked until her body stopped quivering.

"You still with me, Red."

"Yes," was all she said.

"Off." I helped her move, and she plopped down on her stomach beside me. "You can rest while I put on the condom." I reached on the floor and located my jeans, found my wallet, and removed the two condoms I had tucked away. I had a feeling I was going to be glad I picked up a new box by the time I was sated from having her. But for now, the two would have to do. I kicked the sheet away and tore the foil packet open.

"Holy shit, you weren't kidding." Charlie flipped on her back and watched as I rolled the condom on. "You should not have a bird name. They should have named you after a farm animal like bull, horse, stud. I bet other men cry in urinals when you whip that bad boy out."

My lips twitched. The woman held nothing back. "Glad you approve."

85

"Approve! Hell, I'm kinda scared. He looks a little angry."

"I promise, Red, he is anything but angry. And can we not talk about other men and my dick right now?" I rolled over until I laid between her legs and held the majority of my weight on my elbows. I leaned down and met her lips with mine. I ran my tongue over the seam, and when she opened, I pushed my tongue in and explored every crevice. By the time I broke the kiss, Charlie's breaths were coming hard. Her breasts rose with each breath and brought her nipples close enough that they grazed my chest.

My cock throbbed, and I needed inside her in the worst way, but I knew I had to go slow. Just didn't know if I could be gentle, though.

"How many times do I have to tell you, I won't break, Kaden? I'm tougher than I look." Her words, her scent, her taste, everything about her overloaded my senses. The effect had me trailing kisses down her neck until I reached her breasts. I ran my tongue around her nipple and bit gently while I pinched the other nipple between two fingers.

My cock pulsed between us, impatient for the wet warmth that awaited it. I wanted so badly to spread her wide and sink into her. I slid my hands down her body until I reached her thighs, pushing them wider to make room for me.

I slid a finger into her depths and pumped in and out, then added another to stretch her. She was tight but ready as she contracted around my fingers. I pulled them out, and with one arm holding my weight, I reached down with the other and grasped my aching cock, running it through her juices. When the head of my cock rested against her entrance, I took a deep breath and started to push in.

"Christ, your pussy is so tight, I don't know how long I'll last once I get in all the way," I said as I pulled back, then pushed back in, gaining a little ground each time I repeated the motion. The process might have been slow, but when I bottomed out, the feeling of her wrapped tight around my cock felt like home. I gritted my teeth and held still to give her time to adjust to my size.

Charlie's hips lifted, and she started to squirm. "I need you to move, Kaden."

"Impatient are we, Red?" I pulled out and thrust back in. She lifted to meet my downward thrusts until we set a pace that had us both on the brink.

When I felt my balls draw up, I knew I wouldn't last much longer, so I moved a hand between us and pressed down on her clit as I slammed into the hilt, sending us both over the edge.

After we had ridden out the tremors of our orgasms, I pulled out and went and disposed of the condom. When I returned with a warm cloth, Charlie was still on her back, but her eyes were closed.

"You okay?" I asked while I cleaned her. She didn't even move a muscle.

"Tell me we can do that again. Well, after I get my sight back."

I chuckled and tossed the washcloth into the bathroom. "You do know your eyes are closed, right?" As I

87

laid back down on the bed, she turned her head toward me and opened her eyes.

"Thank fuck, I didn't want to give up riding my bike."

I smiled and pulled her into my arms. "And I can guarantee we'll be doing that several more times.

"Hmm…that's a bold statement."

"No, it's a true one. And you will have to deal."

"Bossy is back, but I'm going to let it slide because I'm tired."

"Anything that keeps you from fucking arguing is a win/win for me."

"Asshole."

I smiled. "Rest, and when you wake, we'll do that again."

"To keep me from arguing?"

"No, but do you really care why?"

"No. I'm just glad you bought those condoms." Charlie snuggled into me.

"Me too, Red."

Chapter Seven

Hawk

My eyes opened, and when I looked at the clock, I eased out of bed and made my way to the bathroom. After I showered and went into the bedroom to gather my clothes off the floor and dress, Charlie had yet to move on the bed. Careful not to wake her, I leaned over and gently kissed her forehead.

Once downstairs, I went in search of paper and pen to write her a note. The tablet I found sat on the end table by the couch, and as I grabbed it up, the folder it laid on fell slid off the table, and a photograph drifted across the floor before I could catch it.

"That's a picture of my grandfather." Charlie stepped into the room.

"Sorry, Red. Didn't mean to knock the folder off. I have to leave for Church and was going to leave you a note instead of waking you."

"No big deal, Kaden." She walked over to me and reached for the photo. I handed it over to her, and she stared at it. "Travis has a guy with a copy of this trying to get a hit. And before you ask how he is going to do that, I have no idea. I kinda figured the less I knew, the better." Charlie chuckled and touched the pic with her fingertips.

"That's probably best." I glanced at the photo of the man on the bunk and at everything else that could be seen in the background. Nothing stood out. It could have been any soldier from anywhere. "Too bad the dog tags he's wearing are under the t-shirt."

"That is what Travis and his brothers said. It couldn't be that easy, though. Well...at least not for me anyway."

"Nothing ever is." I placed the notepad on the table, then turned and wrapped Charlie in my arms. Our lips met, and I kissed her. Before the kiss went deeper, I pulled back and let her go. "I wasn't going to leave without telling you. I have Church soon, but I need to run by my house and change my clothes before I head to the clubhouse."

"Okay, no need to explain. I'm going to chill around here and watch some TV today. Thanks for staying and taking care of me. And..."

Damn, it never bothered me before to leave a woman after sex. But the look on Charlie's face put an ache in my chest.

"You want me to pick some food up when I'm done? I could stop back by and chill with you."

"Kaden, you don't have to do that. I'm good. Don't feel like you need to come back because of what we did. I'm a big girl."

How did I tell her that it wasn't the sex, it was her that made me want to come back? No way I'd say that out loud. Instead, I said, "I'll be back."

"I said there was no need to come back. You took care of me. We had sex. It's not a big deal."

I grabbed her face between my hands, tilted her head back and kissed her, then let her go. "Stop trying to cause a fucking argument, it pisses me off." I started toward the door, and she followed me to the garage without a word, and when I had got on my bike, she hit the button to open the door, and after I had backed out, the door closed behind me. I wouldn't be surprised if she didn't answer the door when I showed up again.

I made my way the couple of blocks over to my place, quickly changed my clothes, and was back on my bike headed to the clubhouse in under twenty minutes. After I parked my bike with the others, I walked in and went straight to the prez's office where I found the others sitting around bullshitting.

"Well hell, what got all your asses in here early?" I made my way into the room and took my seat at the table.

"You're in a good mood. Do we owe Charlie thanks for that?" Moose's eyes twinkled and he smirked. I found it amusing, if a little annoying, that he noticed that in me and not himself where Katie was concerned. Haven's Sergeant at

91

Arms smiled and joked a helluva lot more than he had done prior to Katie coming back into his life.

"Like we owe Katie for your warm demeanor." The smirk left Moose's face as he glared at me.

"Girls, can we put the touchy/feely shit away and get down to business," Prez said as he walked in and closed the door. "Moose, you got anything new on Katie's dad's hearing. Then we can go over a change in our plans. I just got a call from General Patel."

"The hearing went well. Looks like Paul is going to end up with probation since he is being cooperative with the FBI. I asked about the human trafficking, and they're working on a few leads to shut it down. They're waiting on the trial dates, but they aren't worried about the convictions, they're solid. Then, of course, Paul is not allowed to hold any job dealing with trading and the SEC. Financially, well, since he can't be attached to anything, my dad is buying him out of the firm. Granted, not going to be the kinda money Paul could have had if he hadn't made those bad investments, but he and Katie's mom will be able to live comfortably."

"I know I've said before, Moose. Anything you need or Katie for that matter. You ask. Okay?"

"Appreciate, Prez."

"Now what type of change in plans are we talking about?" I asked as Prez took his seat.

"They picked up some chatter. It seems whoever made contact with them before has gathered interest, the kind someone doesn't want. New intel is pointing toward the local high school, and they have nothing on who it could be or why, but by what they picked up over the wire, the bad guys know who it is, putting them one up on us already," Prez said and shook his head.

"So, we make up that ground when we get there. Though it could be some high school student, I doubt it. It's more than likely a teacher or one of the other adults who work there. We'll probably have a better chance of locating who is after the person, than the person. Then we use them to find our informer," I said as Prez slid each of us a folder over the table, and I picked mine up.

"That sounds like a job for the best 'Where's Waldo' locator." Keg chuckled, and I flipped him off.

"How about you, Moose? See anything that has been missed that could change the profile for the person?" Prez looked up from his folder and asked.

Moose flipped through the information we were given, then looked up to answer, "I'm going to go with it being a student unless more intel comes in that changes some of this data. I say it's a kid. Intelligent. Excellent grades. He or she is not unsocial, but they're no social butterfly either. He or she knows how to blend in so when people are looking, they look over him or her easily. I noticed the list of students with parents that hold high profile jobs. But did they pull the records of students where the parents have an important job, however, it is one that wouldn't draw unwanted attention yet important enough there could possibly be an issue if someone interfered with the job?" Moose made marks on the papers as he went back to flipping through them.

"Not sure I'm seeing how a kid could have any connection to the woman and four men we're looking to locate before they decide it's time to set their plan in motion. Throw in we don't know what *that* plan is and they could start it and disappear before while it goes through each step they set up, so it has maximum impact." We nodded in agreement with Crank.

"I agree, and that's why I say they should have looked at all the parents' jobs, not just high profile ones," Moose said, though he never looked up from the file in front of him.

"Roach helped me with a couple of listening devices that kept shorting out. So now everything is in working order. We also received a new toy, compliments of General Patel. I took it for a test run while I was out at Roach's place. The brother lives so damn far out with nothing around that it was a perfect place to do the test." Keg had the look of a kid at Christmas.

"Gonna share, brother?" Tram asked.

"Yeah, especially since you will be able to monitor and operate it with the right program on your tablet. We are now in possession of one of the new and recently tested drones the Army has. The bitch is sweet." Keg grinned, and Tram's eyes lit up.

"Okay, now that Christmas came early for Keg and Tram, let's get back to the new development. Pinch?"

"I received the confirmation of the changes for what we need: hotel, car and bike rentals, airfare. We are a go. Even received confirmation that the weapons and things

94

Crank requested will be delivered to the motel to match the earlier arrival time."

We all looked at Wild Bill, and I knew what was coming with Pinch's earlier arrival time.

"Time has been moved up." He looked at his watch and then back around the table, "You got enough time to pack and get to the airport to catch your flights. Taylor and Latch will drive you there. The information on the flight numbers and airlines are the same, it is just the time has changed for this evening. You are still flying out at various times and different airlines in the two-man teams as before. Anyone got any questions?"

We each shook our head and stood.

"Keep me informed and up-to-date when you hit the ground. And I will get in touch with you if anything changes the perimeters of the plan in the slightest while you are in the air. I know I don't have to remind you, but I'm going to anyway. Locate them, but don't confront them unless you are left with no choice. You are to keep an eye on them until Patel's men arrive to move in. Then you get your sorry asses back here. Moose, I'll check in with Katie regularly, and I'll put the new kid on her. I know you're still worried about the blowback from her father's problems. Until we know for sure the FBI has everything taken care of, she will continue to be covered."

"You talking about Yoda?" Moose asked.

Wild Bill shook his head and grinned. "Moose, you really want to stick the kid with that road name if he makes it past prospecting?"

95

"Fuck yeah, it fits him. The kid's always reading some damn philosophy book," I answered before Moose could, and the others agreed.

Prez laughed. "Alright, when the time comes, Yoda it is. I also want to take a vote on Taylor soon, it's time."

"Why don't we vote now? He's going to get a unanimous vote. He's got all the qualities we are looking for. And, Prez, he stayed true through the last round of shit. I vote that his patch is ready to give him when we get back, he's earned it." I looked at the others, and they nodded in agreement.

"Okay, let's do it. Taylor's patch ready and then he'll officially make the switch from prospect to full member after you men get back and we set the time?" Prez asked, got his six resounding 'yes' votes, and Church was officially over when he slapped his gavel down. Before I could stand, Wild Bill asked, "Hawk, can you hold a sec?"

I nodded and stayed seated while the others left to get their things ready. We'd meet up when Taylor and Latch picked us up to take us to the airport.

"You need something before I leave, Prez?"

"No. You heard we are keeping an eye on Katie for Moose. I wanted to ask if we needed us to keep an eye on Charlie?" Prez raised an eyebrow and waited.

It pained me to say it, but I had no claim on Charlie. "No, it's not needed. Thanks for the offer, though. I don't know why you asked, it's not like she's an ol' lady."

"Since this club is just as much yours as mine, Hawk." Wild Bill held his hand up. "It is. From the first time I saw

96

you outside the Roadhouse, there was something about you. I knew after we spoke here in this office, that you would help me make a difference with Haven. You did, and so have the others. Now, I'm going to say something, and you can take my advice or not. There is no timeframe to when you find the right person. A day or a year, it is at your pace and your decision. I met Keg and Sami's mother one night while out with friends, and I had a ring on her finger and Keg on the way before three months passed. You need to do what feels right for you and her."

"I only stayed with her because she needed someone to look after her. That's all."

Wild Bill smirked. "Yeah, keep telling yourself that, maybe then you might believe it. But don't try to blow smoke up my ass on what I witnessed last night when you saw that she was hurt. You and Moose aren't the only ones who can put two and two together. Now go get your things ready. You boys have planes to catch."

I nodded, stood and walked out of the office. By the time I reached my bike, I was focused on the job ahead of us, not who I was leaving behind and would be waiting for me to show back up. No, that would register with me later.

CM Books, LLC

Chapter Eight

Charlie

"Why I am letting this get to me? It's not like I haven't done it myself. I've slept with guys before and then split after. They got what they wanted, and so did I and neither of us had contacted the other or even came back for seconds. Sex had just been sex. No relationship. Nada. And now I am bitching about something I had planned to do to him in the first place. What the fuck is up with that!" I pointed the spatula I was using on the stir-fry at Katie who sat at the table listening to me rant like an insane person.

"Maybe because you feel something for him and want it to mean more. I told you when I got here that they had to leave in a hurry and the reason why Hawk didn't stop by to tell you he was headed out of town."

"Yes, you did. You also won't tell me what the fuck a motorcycle club has going on that would warrant them leaving at the drop of a dime. And might I add, they went on a plane instead of their bikes." I turned the burner off and set the skillet to the side.

"That is for Kaden to tell you, not me. The first thing you are going to have to learn about being with one of these men is that they only tell you what they can, and nothing extra. And if they think they can get by without telling you nothing at all. Well, that is exactly what they will do." Katie took a drink of her tea and set the glass back down on the table before she continued, "Charlie, I've known Kaden as long as you have. I'm just learning about being with a man associated with an MC, the same as you are. They are a different breed of man from at least what I have known prior. Don't forget, I've known Linc most of my life. And though he has always shown some of the qualities I've witnessed with the others, his are ten times as bad now. He's bossier than ever, but it comes from his need to protect. I expect they all carry that quality even as irritating as it is."

I pulled the plates down from the cabinet shelf and sat them on the counter and reached for the skillet before I replied, "So they are jerks who turn into major assholes when you get them in a group?"

Katie laughed as she got up and grabbed the plates, taking them to the table after I placed food on them. I snagged the silverware and joined her.

"I guess that is one way to look at it. Not sure they have to be in a group to come off as jerks. However, I'd rather look at it as—they care so much it makes them extra-protective, which then makes them extra-assholish when stuff doesn't go their way. They are gruff, rude at times, bitchier than any female suffering PMS, pushy, but they are also the most loyal, tender when you least expect it from them, caring, and they will always put your needs first—even if they are the only ones who see it as your need. An example of what that means is the prospect out front. I may not think I need him, but Moose evidently does. If it makes him relax, then having a tail is a minor inconvenience I can deal with. It didn't seem to bother you, you're the one who fixed an extra plate for him."

"Ah, but Mac is a cutie." We both burst out laughing. I'd noticed the young guy parked in front of my place when I let Katie in.

"Yes, he is, and young, which is why he turned fifteen shades of red from the neck up when you yelled from the door to ask him if he wanted to come in and join two cougars for dinner."

"Hey, at least I asked if you knew someone was watching you instead of my first thought of it being someone associated with your dad's mess. I was going to excuse myself once we went into the kitchen, then sneak up on him, and zap his ass with my stun gun." I shrugged and took a bite of food.

"Well, I'm glad you asked me. I would have hated having to explain to Moose or the others why Mac was incapacitated."

"True."

We finished eating in silence and then took our plates to the sink. Katie started rinsing them off as I wiped off the counters. It'd been a while since I'd spent time with a female friend.

"So…are you going to cut Kaden a break when he gets back?" Katie asked as she loaded the dishes in the dishwasher, then closed it.

I took a deep breath, then blew it out. "Maybe if he shows up and is somewhat sorry for not even taking a minute to drop by and let me know he was heading out of town. I mean, I know he doesn't have my number so I can't blame him for not calling. But, Katie, who says he had any intention of coming back. He could have just said he was because he thought I'd make a scene. Though I'm not sure why considering I told him he didn't have to."

"I call bullshit. If he said he was coming back, he planned to do it. That's something else about the men, they don't waste words. Heck, they definitely never waste time with niceties. I saw with my eyes how Kaden looks at you. And he may not say it, which falls under wasted words as I mentioned before, he will show you with his actions. Linc is like that, too. I bet most of the men are."

"Alright. I guess we shall see when he gets back. Now, let's take cutie pie, Mac, his plate out and see how many more shades of red we can get him to turn."

Katie placed foil over the plate while I grabbed Mac a drink out of the fridge. "So…I'm taking that since you are considering giving Kaden the benefit of the doubt, the sex was better than good?"

102

I couldn't help it, I laughed. Katie was trying to lighten the conversation. "Well, girlfriend, what do you think? You sleep with one of them."

Katie stopped on the sidewalk and turned with a huge smile on her face. "Why, yes. Yes, I do."

I raised my free hand up and she high-fived me, then we both burst out laughing. When we continued down the driveway, we noticed a motorcycle with no rider parked behind the truck. When we started to cross the street, Wild Bill stepped out of the passenger side of Mac's truck and that brought a new round of giggles from Katie and me.

"Ladies." Wild Bill leaned against the truck and smiled.

When I noticed the windows were down in the truck, it made me wonder how much the two men might have heard as Katie and I stepped out of my place. I bent and looked in the truck, and the hint of pink on Mac's face gave me my answer. Wild Bill's next words only confirmed it.

"The men of Haven aim to please. Glad to hear the men make you happy."

"Umm...well...thanks. We were just bringing Mac something to eat. We would have brought you a plate if we'd known you were going to be here." Katie's stammering had Wild Bill smile growing, and I couldn't help but snicker, which drew a glare from Katie.

"There's more in the house if you'd like some, Wild Bill?" I asked.

"Thanks, sweetheart, but already ate. I just came by to see how Mac was fairing. I see he is being taken care of."

"Mac is a cutie pie. We invited him in to have dinner, but he declined," I said as Katie walked around the truck and handed Mac the plate and drink. The blush he had going on had gone from pink to a nice shade of red at my words. Mac must have shared that information with Wild Bill because he chuckled as he pushed off the truck.

"Take it easy on my new prospect. And he was wise to decline the invite to dinner. Mac's young, but he doesn't lack for brains, and I'm sure he likes his balls where they are. And if Moose and Hawk got a hold of them, they wouldn't be much use to him. Remember he is here to protect you if the need arises and he'd do it with his life, any of the men would. So…don't put him in unnecessary danger." Wild Bill walked to his bike and got on, but before he started it, he spoke to Katie, "Latch or Taylor will relieve Mac in the morning, Katie. The three will be rotating, so one of them will be close at all time. You need anything, you call. Hear me?"

"Thanks, Wild Bill but you don't have to—" Katie was cut off, and the argument stopped before it began as I got a firsthand glimpse of why Wild Bill was the president of Haven MC. His mouth lost the earlier smile that relaxed his facial features to a thin line and a facial feature that said he'd take no argument on the matter.

"Your job is not to worry about your safety. It's Moose and the clubs. The men are on you whether you like it not. You want to argue? Save it for Moose, he's obligated to listen. I'm not. And, Charlie, I think you might want to adhere to what I said. That way you know what's ahead for you, too."

"Excuse me, I'm not sure that's going to be necessary."

The smile was quick on his face as he looked at me. "We'll see. Here's a little something for you to remember, though. We're men and we like having things our way. When we don't get it, it takes us by surprise, then we tend to overreact. Plus, it takes a couple fuck-ups for us to get it right most times. So give Hawk a break. My men are used to dealing with other people's feelings, not their own. Have a nice night, ladies." Wild Bill had his bike cranked and was halfway down the street before I found my voice.

"Well damn, I've never seen that no-nonsense side of him before. It's kinda sexy. In an older man if I didn't already have a younger one who was hung that I was trying to decide if I wanted in my corner way."

Katie grinned and shook her head, and I actually thought I heard Mac chuckle, either that, or he was choking on the food. I glanced in the window and saw him grinning as he shoveled food in his mouth.

"Dude, if you so much as tell what you just heard, you'll find out that Moose and Hawk aren't the only ones who can put you out of commission. And I'll make sure that Katie and I call you Cutie Pie around as many of Haven's members as we can so when they tag you with a road name, Cutie Pie will stick."

Katie placed her arm through mine and started to usher me back to the house. And I was sure she regretted telling me some of the basics on how an MC worked.

"Ma'am?" I turned Katie and I around when Mac spoke.

"What? And it's Charlie."

Mac grinned and it was lethal to a woman's senses. "Ma'am," he placed emphasis on the word, "you might want to remember that I'm a prospect in an MC. We do whatever jobs the leadership tells us to do. Ones that no one else wants to do. You know…like bury bodies."

Katie burst out laughing, and I stared at the young man who now wore a smirk on his face.

I grinned. "Nice one, dude. I think you're going to do just fine. I like you, Cutie Pie." He groaned as I turned and headed with Katie to the house.

After we settled in, we talked, watched a movie, then Mac followed Katie home. I locked up and set the alarm, went up to my room and climbed in my bed. As I started to fall asleep, I wondered where Kaden was spending his night.

Chapter Nine

Charlie

"Hey, my brothers from a different mother. I brought donuts." The guys were at their desks and looked up when I walked into the office.

"What the hell, are you drunk?" Josh asked as I sat the box of donuts on top his desk.

I walked to my desk and flopped down in my chair. "Nope, just happy."

"I think I like you better bitchy," Jake said as he rolled his chair over to Josh's desk and lifted the lid on the box, grabbing a donut.

"Ah, is it that time of the month for someone." I laughed when Jake glared at me.

"See, now if one of us had said anything about your rag when you were acting bitchy, you would've been screaming harassment or some other kind of bullshit like that," Mitchell said as he did the same with his chair and rolled over to get a donut.

Travis was the only one who actually got up out of his chair and walked to get his. "Can we please not talk about *anyone's* rag, male or female?" Travis took his donut and went back to his desk.

"Geez, I would think after being at Haven's party Saturday night. One, I might add, that had women present who are known to put out, you boys would be in much better moods." I looked at each of them, knowing out of the four of them, Josh was the one who would spill all.

He turned his chair to face me and pointed the half-eaten donut in his hand at me. "Let me tell ya, it would have been better if some of them hadn't spoken first." I grinned, and he continued, "Now that wasn't me complaining, 'cause we all know I don't have any standards. If she is breathing and puts out, hell, I'll tap it. Travis is the one who likes his women to be able to converse and not the 'fuck me, baby, harder, faster,' conversing, with actual sentences using more than one syllable words."

Travis groaned, then said, "There were two of you. I don't understand why Mom insisted on keeping you both. She should have given you up for adoption, Josh."

I'd noticed since I started working with the brothers that they may look almost identical, but their personalities were far from it. Josh was the one who didn't seem to let much bother him.

Josh waved off Travis, "Please, I'm the baby. She loves me more than you three."

"Seriously, asshole, I was only born six minutes ahead of you," Jake said and flipped Josh off. Growing up in their home had to be a riot. Well, probably not for their parents.

"Six minutes cost you the baby spot in the family and our mother's undying love." I laughed as wadded up paper flew at Josh from his brothers as he dodged and continued, "Now back to our different moods and what standards are expected for us to get laid. Travis's mood is typical of a male who did not get laid Saturday night because his standards are too high." A pen went flying by Josh's head, and he laughed. "Mitchell, well his mood is reflective of a man who got relief by the temporary kind, because he too, like Travis, seems to think a woman should be able to talk for him to reach maximum relief. However, he stepped out of his regular zone, to give his hand a break. Plus, a blowjob does keep the woman nonverbal, it just doesn't have the same effect as rocking the bed sex."

I was laughing so hard tears escaped the corners of my eyes. And Mitchell launched a notepad like a Frisbee, narrowly missing Josh's head.

"And Jake...well... I love him because he is my other half, but other than our shared looks and our eight and a half months of living in tight quarters together, we are vastly different in how we approach sex. Where I don't care how I'm getting it, as long as I'm getting it, type of guy. Jake is we can do it, but it is always my way because you secretly like that way and want to serve me, type of guy." Jake wheeled his chair back to Josh's desk, popped the back of his head

109

and wheeled back to his desk with the box of donuts. I laid my forehead on my desk and continued to laugh.

"Now, you, my friend, are a—"

I raised my head and looked at Josh, who was grinning from ear-to-ear. "Oh, this outta be good." I leaned back in my chair no longer laughing at the expense of the other brothers since Josh felt the need to include me in his craziness.

"Ah, no need for thanks, my dear. You are a see it, want it, go get it, and no apology type girl." Josh cocked his brow. "Am I right so far?"

"What if you are? There's nothing wrong with that." I crossed my arms over my chest and glared back.

"Not at all, but it's changed."

"Are you sure you aren't the drunk one? What the fuck are you talking about it changed?"

The office phone rang, and Travis answered, and while he talked to whoever was on the other end, I waited to be woo wooed by Josh's insight.

"Well, after the display of 'I Tarzan, you Jane' by the hunky VP of Haven the other night and your happy ass walking in here today. I'd say you liked swinging from his little rope enough to give up some control. And for you to do that, you trusted him enough to know he won't let you fall." Josh stood, then bent over in a show of taking a bow. I grabbed the local phone book on my desk and threw it at him before he rose, hitting him in the back of his head. Mitchell and Jake laughed, and Travis glared and put his hand over the receiver and told us to be quiet.

I lowered my voice, "Well, I don't usually share private stuff, but...there is nothing *little* about Kaden." Josh slammed his head on his desk and groaned. "But I do wonder what Kaden would think of you referring to him as the hunky VP."

Josh raised his head and smirked. "You don't know, he might like it. How well do you know him?"

I burst out laughing at the absurdity that was Josh, earning me another glare from Travis as he ended the call.

Travis pulled the page off the notepad he'd been writing on and walked over and sat it on my desk. When I picked it up and read what was written, every emotion imaginable ran through my system. I looked up at Travis, and he grinned.

"Seriously?" I felt tears form in my eyes, and when I went to wipe them, I cringed when I rubbed a little too hard across my bruised cheek.

"Yeah, hun. My contact is a hundred percent sure." The other brothers were now standing beside my desk, so I turned the paper around so they could read it.

"Son-of-a-bitch," was said simultaneously by the three of them.

"You going to be okay, Charlie? It's what you wanted to find out, right?" Josh asked all previous joking set aside.

"Yes, I'll be fine. It's just that a part of me thought he would be deceased. I prepared for that, so if it were true, I wouldn't be disappointed. Do you understand?" The brothers nodded. "And now to have it confirmed that grandfather is living, in the same area, it's surreal."

CM Books, LLC

"Now that this is real. What are you going to do if he isn't receptive to you, darlin'?" Mitchell asked.

"Oh, I expect him to be shocked, hurt even, hell...I was. Other than that, I'll accept what he decides to do with the information. If he is acceptable to the information, then that is on him."

"Do you want to leave now, Charlie?" Travis asked, then added, "We'll go with you if you need us to?"

I thought about the offer because I knew the brothers would go with me if nothing more than to give me support. "I think I will go ahead a leave, but I think I need to do this on my own. Though I do appreciate the offer." I stood, folded the paper and put it in my pocket, then grabbed my phone and keys off my desk.

"Take a few days if you need to, Charlie. We got nothing going on right now. And good luck," Travis said and patted my shoulder. I headed for the door before he could change his mind, or I changed mine. This was why I'd taken the job and moved across the country.

The ride across town seemed to take forever, but it gave me time to settle my nerves. When I pulled up to the gate, I smiled at the man who stood guard.

"Don't they let you sleep, Cutie Pie?" Mac's expression didn't change, and I was surprised that he didn't even blush.

"What do you need, ma'am?"

"I thought we had this discussion. The name is Charlie, Cutie Pie."

"Yes, we did. So, what can I do for you...ma'am?" The twitching of his lips gave him away.

"Ah, you think you're funny, huh?" I had to bite the inside of my cheek to keep from laughing. I really did like the young man.

"Someone has to be." Mac's face when he answered, was so blank of emotion, I almost lost my fight and laughed.

"Hey, I'm funny." I gave him the most serious face I could muster.

His brow lifted. "No, you really are not." That reply did it, and I laughed.

I held up my hands. "I give. I don't know why people don't think I'm funny. But whatever. I came to see Wild Bill. Is he in... Mac?"

"Let me text him... Charlie." He pulled out his phone and punched the buttons. It didn't take long for his phone to beep with a reply. Mac didn't say another word, he pulled the gate opened, stepped to the side and waved me in. I rolled the bike forward until I was right beside him, then I stopped.

"You can be a little assholish. You're going to fit right in at Haven." I moved the bike forward but not before I saw a grin spread across Mac's face.

Other than a few bikes, the lot was empty. I backed into a spot beside the door, and when I dismounted and turned, the door opened, and Wild Bill walked out.

"Thanks for seeing me, Wild Bill," I said and walked toward him.

"Not a problem. Something you need, Charlie?"

113

"Sort of. I'm not sure how much you know about me. I took the job with the Matherson brothers because they are good at what they do, but I also made the move to look for my grandfather."

"Yeah, I heard about that. I don't know what Haven can do to help, but if you tell me what you need, I'll definitely see what we can do." Instead of answering him, I reached into my pocket and handed him the piece of paper.

Wild Bill unfolded the paper and began reading. I watched his face, but he gave nothing away. When he finished, he folded the paper back up and held on to it, then he turned toward the door. "Come in, Charlie. Let's go to my office and discuss this."

"Sure. Is there something wrong?" I asked as he held the door open for me. Wild Bill's face was unreadable. I walked in with Wild Bill behind me just as an older man I hadn't seen before stepped out of the main room.

"Hey, Prez. I was looking for you. Got some lunch ready in the kitchen if you want some. Plenty if your guest wants to join you, too."

"Thanks, Roach. I'll grab a little something in a few. Have you met Charlie, Roach?"

The man looked me over, then smiled. "Ah, Hawk's redhead. Nope, I haven't had the pleasure. Nice to meet you, Charlie." Roach stuck out his hand, and I shook it, wondering if there was anyone in the club that didn't know about Hawk and me.

"Charlie and I are going to my office to go over something. Can you join us?" Wild Bill asked.

Roach frowned. "Yeah, you need me to help with something, Prez?"

I watched the two men as they spoke to each other. People always seemed to jump to the wrong conclusions when they saw bikers because they judged them by their outer appearance instead of getting to know them. I'm sure under the right circumstance or the wrong, depending on how it's looked at, they could be scary as hell. But in the short time I'd been around Haven MC, the men were friendly, loyal to one another, and willing to help with no questions asked if they considered you a friend.

"Yeah, I want you to look at something." Roach never questioned, he followed Wild Bill, and so did I.

When we entered the office, Wild Bill waved at the seats in front of his desk as he took the one behind it.

"So, what do you want me to look at?" Roach asked as he took the seat beside me.

"Did you hear that Charlie was looking for her grandfather?" Wild Bill asked.

"Yeah, Hawk mentioned it. He said the Matherson brothers were helping with it."

"I got something I want you to take a look at and tell me what you think." Wild Bill unfolded the paper and handed it to Roach. I didn't say anything because I figured Wild Bill wanted Roach to take a look because he was one of the older ones in the club and probably knew the man.

Roach took the paper and started reading. His expression never changed as he read the name and that the man was associated with Haven MC. I wondered if the men in the club knew how similar their actions were. When he was done, he glanced at Wild Bill, then at me.

"Is this for real?" Roach waved the paper for emphasis.

"Yes. Travis's contact said that was the name of Charlie's grandfather. Do you happen to know Spencer Danson?" Wild Bill grinned. "The contact didn't have anything else other than he was associated with Haven. Probably would have made it easier if he had come up with a road name. Don't you think?"

I looked at Wild Bill, then Roach. Both men's faces had softened, and Roach smiled back at Wild Bill. "Yeah, that would have helped."

Roach turned and looked at me. "What's your grandmother's name, Charlie?"

"Annette Rhoades," I said.

Roach's eyes took on a faraway look, then he whispered, "Annie."

"Yes, that is what her friends called her. Did you know her, too?" I asked, the excitement in my voice noticeable in my own ears.

Roach focused back in on me. "Charlie, I'm Spencer Danson."

I felt the tears form in my eyes as I looked at Roach. I couldn't stop them. The more I studied his face, I saw that my dad shared some of his features: the square jawline, his nose, and the same warm brown eyes. I wondered briefly if I had met Roach before Travis's contact found a name if I would have seen the resemblance to my dad as I had between with the photo of the young soldier.

Roach cleared his throat. "I have so many questions, Charlie. Some I can guess at the answer. Like Annie being pregnant when she left here. I didn't know. She never told me. I guessing since your last name is Rhoades, she had a son. What I don't understand is why you had to search for me. I've haven't left this area since I came back from the military. Why didn't she give you my name?"

"My grandmother died over a year ago." The sadness and hurt that crossed over Roach's face had my tears spilling over. "I'm so sorry. She never told my dad who his father was. We never knew your name. There was only a picture of a soldier laying on a bunk. Nothing was even written on the back. It's the one I used to find you. Well, not me, Travis's contact."

Wild Bill got up and went across the room and brought a box of tissues back and handed them to me. I nodded my thanks and pulled one out of the box and dabbed at my eyes.

"Grandmother had a stroke, which stole a lot of her memories and impaired her speech. She struggled at the end to relay something to us. I figured out it was about you. She said Washington as the place you lived when I asked. Then she'd talk about a biker. It was bits and pieces that seemed to pop into her head at random times. Before she could heal from the first stroke, another hit her, and it hit her hard. She stayed with us for a few days, but she didn't survive the last one."

"Well wasn't that awful for her."

"What?" I stared at the man who was my grandfather.

"I miss years of my son growing up, years of you growing up because *she* chose not to talk about me until she had death knocking at her door!"

I swallowed and wiped at the tears running down my cheeks. How could I feel happiness from locating my grandfather, and sad because of the lost years?

I knew what Roach was feeling, and I felt so bad for him. He was facing what my father and I had when she died. We'd both asked the same questions to each other. Why did she wait until the end?

"I can't do this." Roach stood, walked to and out the door with Wild Bill getting up and going after him.

I sat there for a few minutes, wiped my eyes, and blew my nose. I rose, set the box of tissues on Wild Bill's desk and walked out of the office, out of the clubhouse, then rode out of the parking lot. Never once looking back.

When I reached my house, I went into the living room and sat down on the couch. Pulling the photo out of the folder, I studied it, refusing to believe that I had found and lost my grandfather all in one day. Life could be that cruel, could it? Roach would come around; it was just a shock to him as it had been for my dad and me. Even a bigger one for him since he never knew he'd had a child. What had my grandmother been thinking for all those years?

My cell rang startling me, and I picked it up and glanced at the screen. It was a number I didn't recognize, but

I hit the button and answered anyway. The distraction for even a minute would be appreciated.

"Hello," I answered and expected to hear some spiel from a salesman, credit card company or my favorite, the scammers posing as the IRS telling you that you needed to pay, or they were coming for you. What jerks? I hadn't expected the voice that came over the line.

"Hey, Red. How are you doing?" Kaden asked, and I burst into tears. "Whoa, Red. What is going on? Has something happened?"

I swiped at the tears flowing from my eyes but couldn't control the sobs.

"Come on, baby. You're scaring me. What the fuck happened?" Kaden's voice was urgent, and I worked on getting myself under control.

"I... I located...my...grand...father," I said between sobs. I couldn't even rationalize why I was crying.

"Umm...Red, shouldn't you happy? Wasn't that what you wanted? Help me understand, baby."

Taking deep breaths, I worked to pull myself together. Kaden waited quietly on the other end of the phone.

"I'm sorry. I don't know why I'm crying. You know, with finding the picture and wondering if we would even find him... Through it all, I've had time to absorb the shock, and everything else in dealing with this. I knew if I found him, he would need the same time and I was willing to give it, but actually being there, I don't know. When he said he couldn't do it and walked out, all that understanding left and it just...hurt, Kaden. I've wondered my whole life and to have him leave…"

"Your grandfather walked out on you? Christ, Red, I'm the one who's sorry. Sorry, you had to deal with it by yourself. I should have been there. Don't worry, okay? When I get back, I'll deal with the man. What a prick."

I held the phone out and looked down at the screen, and the whole pot and kettle thing made me smile. At least I hadn't lost my humor.

"Kaden, thank you for the offer, but you probably are going to want to reevaluate your offer to help."

"I doubt that. Why do you think I would?" Kaden sounded almost offended at my suggestion.

"Kaden, my grandfather is Roach." The line went quiet, and I checked to be sure we hadn't gotten disconnected.

"No, shit? Fucking talk about coincidences. Christ, Red. I don't even know what to say. But if you need me to, I will give him a smack to his head."

"Thanks. And yeah, he evidently didn't know what to say either." I went on and explained everything that had happened, and Kaden listened without responding until I finished.

"Red, I'm not saying that didn't happen. It's just Roach wouldn't act like that. Baby, maybe the shock was too much, and he will come around when it sinks in. Damn, I wish the fuck I was there."

Kaden's words reminded me that he wasn't there and also of something else. "Kaden, how did you get my number? Plus, I shouldn't even be talking to you for standing me up."

I was over the pity-party and chose to change the subject. I didn't know what any of this meant with Kaden calling me, but like Katie and I had discussed—it was up to me if I thought there could be something between Kaden and me.

"I had Moose get it from Katie. I wanted to call to let you know I didn't blow you off. I had every intention of coming back to your place. It was just that something came up."

"Where are you at, Kaden?"

"Can't tell you that, Red. And before you go off on a rant, I'm going to go ahead and let you know that there are things I will not talk to you about. Club business and the work I do for it. There is something between us. I haven't figured it out, but I want to. You're going to have to decide if you can deal with not knowing my every move. It's up to you, Red."

"So I can't ask any questions? I won't put up with other women, Kaden. I'm not made that way. When I'm with someone, I don't share."

"Red, I'm talking club business. You can ask questions; it just depends if I can answer them. And I sure as fuck wasn't talking about other women. Goddammit, I haven't touched another woman since the day you came to my place. I might be the asshole you claim me to be, but I'm not a cheater, Red. Now, with Roach being your grandad, might be hard if you decide you don't want a relationship

CM Books, LLC

with me. I mean, we are going to run into each other, but I won't call you or come by again if you're not interested." There was silence between until Kaden whispered, "Can you trust me, baby?"

Could I? When I thought about it, the answer came quickly because part of me already did.

"Yes," I whispered back.

"Yeah? Well good. Now tell me what other kinda trouble you've gotten into since I've been gone."

"You've only been gone a day, Kaden."

"And your point, Red." I could hear the humor in his voice and imagined he wore a smirk on his face to go with it.

We talked and laughed, and by the time I got off the phone, I felt better. Relaxed and with my resolve back to give Roach time to deal with the information I dumped on him. I made the first contact, now the next move was going to have to be his. I would have to bide my time and hope he came around.

Chapter Ten

Hawk

"Fucking crotch rocket. Really?" Keg's bitching came through the earpiece.

"How many times are you going to mention the damn bike? Get over it," Moose answered and shook his head.

"As many times as the damn seat on this thing pinches my balls, I'm may never be able to make kids," Keg continued to bitch, and chuckles could be heard from the others through the earpieces.

"What arc you doing on the seat? I'm on the same kinda bike, and though I would rather be on my Harley Fatboy, this thing isn't bothering me," Pinch said. He and Keg were on Suzuki Hayabusas that were positioned and pointing in either direction to be able to take over the tail if Moose and I needed them to.

"All that means is my dick is bigger, and these seats aren't made for such large sizes." I pinched between my eyes because I knew the response from Keg would set Pinch off.

"Fuck you, dickhead. The only thing you got bigger is your mouth."

Pinch and Keg had been going back and forth since we met up with them at the motel. The most any of us made out of it, was Keg had asked Pinch how his sister was doing as they were in route to meet us at the motel. Pinch evidently was having none of it. We had a bet going (unbeknownst to Pinch) on how long Madison would let her brother keep her from associating with the club before she bucked against his rule about her not attending any of the parties. It had been an ongoing fight between the two of them since she'd come of age. But since she'd been of age for several years, I wondered if the argument was out of habit.

"Fifteen minutes until the dismissal bell. Any update on our friends?" I asked.

"Nah. They're still just sitting in the SUV. Tram's linked into the GPS Keg slapped on the vehicle yesterday," Crank said. He and Tram were in one vehicle on one end of the block while Moose and I were at the other end of the block. The two men in the SUV had been in their spot since we arrived, which had been an hour ago.

"Hey, that's two of the four men we had to look for. With any luck, they'll lead to the others and we can wrap this shit up. Because honest to God, I don't know how they've stayed hidden so long. Other than they don't have to hide now because time is about up on what they have planned," I said, and the others groaned.

"Shit, VP, you probably jinxed us," Keg came through the earbud.

Moose, Crank, Tram, and I arrived at BOS (Boston Logan International Airport) just after five thirty yesterday morning, on separate airlines, while Keg and Pinch departed at a different time, arriving a couple hours behind us. The vehicles were picked up, and the bikes were in the parking lot of the motel with the keys in the rooms along with everything we requested.

The email from Wild Bill with additional intel obtained while we were in the air, greeted Tram when he signed on his computer. We studied it and made the necessary adjustments to our plans while we waited for Pinch and Keg to arrive.

We spent the day familiarizing ourselves with the area. At least as well as we could in one day. The day hadn't been wasted because it gave us the opportunity to drive by the school as they were letting out so we could take note of the directions the buses headed and where a good place would be for us to set up. Our payoff for our effort was the two assholes that sat down the road. They'd been in the same spot yesterday.

Sleeper cells were the worst in my book. The individuals laid in wait for months, even years, setting up for that one shock and awe that could devastate the country. They watched, they timed, and then they struck. The individuals blend into the background and go unnoticed, never drawing attention to themselves, which made them even harder to find.

I'd figured out the difference between them and the random acts of terrorism. It boiled down to patience, which

125

contributed to the effect of the attack. With random ones, it always happens quickly. They never seemed to have the best laid out plans. It was if they had a thought and days, or a few weeks at the most, they acted.

The only thing similar in the two was whatever was done resulted in some type of devastation and death, just on a different scale. The one common thing shared between them that I'd seen—the willingness to die to obtain their results. Making them very dangerous.

Our job was to find, identify, and force them out of hiding. Hopefully, before the plan the fuckers had was in the works or executed. Then we faded into the background while the sweeper team collected them, leaving our identities shielded and unknown to strike another day.

I looked at my watch. "We are down to two minutes. Everyone needs to pay attention. Keg, Pinch, you still good?"

"Yeah, Hawk, I'm good. Sitting on the side of the road pretending to talk on my cell phone, which I gotta add that some rude ass people live here because not one fucker has stopped to ask if I was broke down or needed help," Keg ranted.

Moose groaned beside me, and I shook my head. There was no sense in us replying, Keg would bitch if they had stopped and called them nosey fuckers. When the brother was tired, he turned into a major dick and bitched about everything.

"I'm good, Hawk. Haven't moved from the edge of that shopping center parking lot we scoped out yesterday.

126

It's a quarter-mile away from the school, but still close enough for me to react if necessary," Pinch answered.

"We're good, too, and our friends have started their vehicle. Guess they want to be able to move without delay," Crank checked in, and the sound of the bell could be heard, then kids started to pour out the doors of the school.

"Nah, I'm going with they are posted to make sure whoever the kid is, doesn't leave the school building once they are here," Moose replied.

I glanced at Moose, then back to the kids either walking away or getting on the buses.

"Why?" I asked.

"They would have grabbed them already. I think they suspect him or her, but they don't have enough proof to be one hundred percent. Or getting rid of them would bring too much focus their way, which tells me someone the kid knows has to be involved. We know we were to locate four men and a woman. Two of the men sit in that vehicle, which means the kid doesn't know them because they aren't worried about being seen. Now we have the numbers narrowed down to two men and the woman missing in action. For now, anyway," what Moose said made a helluva lot of sense.

The kids started to thin out. Buses pulled away, and several groups of kids walked off together. The kids I focused on were the ones who stayed to themselves.

"Kids are dwindling down. Are the two men still in the car, Crank?" I asked.

"Yeah, they're still in the same spot. But they're looking up and down the street as if maybe they lost them," Crank answered, and it made sense. Because if the kid slipped by them, it could cost them the only opportunity they have, depending on their schedule.

The front doors of the school opened again and a group of kids piled out with computer bags thrown over their shoulders. Normal looking kids with nothing about them that stood out. As they talked a car pulled up and the group turned, then one of the boys walked toward it. The tinted windows made it hard to get an identifying visual on who was inside, but I could make out it was a woman with long hair.

"Crank, Tram, can you see the driver of that car?" I asked and filled Keg and Pinch in on the kid and the woman.

"No, but the two men who were waiting are on the move, heading in your direction," Tram said, and I could even hear his fingers tapping the keys on his laptop. Moose turned his attention to the road while I watched the kid.

The boy opened the car and bent down to look inside but didn't get in. He talked with the driver while the car carrying the two men passed by. If I hadn't been watching so closely, I probably would have missed the slight turn of the man's head who was driving toward the car and then the over the shoulder glance by the woman in the car at the curb.

As Moose and I watched the interaction of the woman and kid, Crank and Tram drove past, following the vehicle with the two men in it. The boy stood and shook his head in answer to whatever the driver said, and then he closed the

128

car door. He stayed watching as the car pulled away, then I saw him sneer before he turned and walked toward the group who were heading down the sidewalk away from the school.

"Keg, the woman is headed in your direction. She's driving a late model black Camry with tinted windows. Pinch, ride toward Keg and you two follow her. Moose and I will tail the kid while Crank and Tram stay with the men. Keep your eyes open. I don't know what this woman and kid mean, but if she is involved, that still leaves two men out there we haven't tagged yet. We don't need any surprises."

Everyone acknowledged, and I pulled the SUV out onto the street to tail the kid. We were either going to be lucky or waste some time.

Damn, I would welcome some luck.

We sat in the back of the restaurant we had planned as a meeting place. The angle of the table gave us an open view of the entrance, along with privacy to talk. The briefing of what each of us found was held off until the waitress sat our orders down on the table and walked off.

"Keg and I tailed the woman to a carrier business downtown and circled a few times. Nothing unusual about the place. A few bike carriers pulled out, even a few trucks pulled around back of the place, which I assume were coming in for the day from deliveries." Pinch picked up his silverware, then continued," The woman is young, maybe late twenties, early thirties. Not old enough to have a kid that is seventeen or eighteen, though. She was foreign, and yes, she looked to be from the Middle East." I knew Pinch was finished when he started to eat.

"Our boys went back to the apartment we drove by yesterday. We parked down the street and watched for a bit to see if they came back out. The tall, thin one came out after about ten minutes and headed up the street on foot. We tailed him to a convenience store. When some time passed, and he didn't come out, I got out and walked in. It's where he works because he was behind the counter. We already know both the men are from the Middle East." I cocked a brow at Tram, and he smiled. "Yeah, yeah a lot of people are from the Middle East but in our world and I'm talking club. When have you come across three, not related as per our intel, with various positions near each other?"

"True but other than that, we have nothing else that ties them together. The kid went with the others to a coffee shop in the shopping center were Pinch was parked. He sat at a table with the others, and they ordered drinks and opened their computers. They sat and worked for an hour, then we followed him to a medium income neighborhood. Nice house, well taken care of, but it was an older home," Moose said and took a drink of the beer he ordered with his dinner.

I picked up my glass of water and took a drink. "Okay, not much, but more than we had yesterday. When we get back to the motel, Tram, start working on the carrier business and the house address for the kid."

"I'll get on it as soon as we get back," Tram said, and the conversation stopped while we demolished the steak dinners.

Back at the rooms, Tram opened his laptop and got down to business, shutting the rest of us out while he did his thing. The others sat around and talked, and I took a break to check in with Prez.

"How's it going for you boys, Hawk?"

"Hey, Prez. Might already have a break. At least we hope so." I informed Wild Bill of everything that happened since we arrived.

"So, you got the woman and two of the men? Any info on where the other two are hiding?"

"Negative on the other two. Tram is searching right now for more info. Not sure on the woman yet. Just a gut feeling. Should know something soon. I'd feel better if I knew where those other two were, though."

"Only been two days, Hawk. You'll locate them. It's different being away when someone is waiting for you at home, isn't it?"

"She's under my skin, that's for sure. Has Roach been by to see her?"

Wild Bill went quiet, and then I heard him sigh. "You've talked with her. No. I went by Roach's place today because he hasn't even come by the club. He was home, yelled through the door he was fine. Told me he needed some time to himself. He'll figure it out, Hawk, and then I imagine he will reach out to Charlie."

"Yeah, I called her before my plane left. I'm glad I did. He goddamn better reach out to her. Roach isn't the only one hurting, Prez. Charlie is, too. He needs to pull his head out of his ass before I get back and shove in further." Prez's chuckle caught me off guard. "What the hell, Prez? Nothing about this is funny."

"Oh, calm down, Hawk. First Moose, now you. I may not survive the rest of you pairing off. And Keg scares me the worst."

"Well, he is your son, Prez."

"There is that. But, Christ, you and Moose have chosen some pretty impressive women. Keg, though—I will be surprised if she'll be able to add two and two. His track record hasn't been that great since his high school sweetheart moved east."

"He might surprise you?"

"One can only hope."

The motel door opened, and I looked over my shoulder, and Moose motioned with his head.

"Gotta go, Prez. I'll check in later."

"Do that. You boys stay safe."

I hung up and walked back into the motel room. The guys stood behind Tram while he pointed to different things on his computer screen.

"What is that?" I asked as I walked up beside Moose and glanced at the screen.

"This is the computer system for the carrier business the woman went to today." Tram looked over his shoulder at me.

"Okay, what are we looking at? And do I want to know how you got into their system?"

"Through the backdoor. They didn't have a lock on it." Tram chuckled at his own computer joke. "Let me go to the beginning and I will show you."

Data moved across the screen that to me was totally unreadable. To Tram, though, it was second nature, he focused on the screen, and his fingers moved over the keypad. I looked around at the others and they were watching, too. Tram could have made a killing as a hacker. Anytime we've needed him, he has gotten the information. We hadn't come across a program he couldn't crack. It was astounding to watch.

"Like I said, I got in through the backdoor. Nice, expensive system and cheap ass security. I will never understand why businesses do that. Anyway, once I was in, I was able to follow a route to each computer on the system: shipping, admin, payroll. Got to say some of the employees there don't make dick. Sad, 'cause the company is raking in the green. Here," Tram pointed at the screen that came up, "this is a log of everything they picked up and delivered."

Tram went over a couple more shipping logs, then briefly showed the payroll and company expenses. Next came the list of clients that used the carrier company. The list was long.

"They do pick up and deliveries for just about every type of company: law offices, pharmaceutical companies to hospitals, doctors' offices, clinics, a few labs. Now here is the shipping clerk's computer." Tram brought up a screen with data notations that I had no clue what they were.

"What the hell is all that?" Moose asked what I was thinking.

"This is where everything starts to get interesting. What you are looking at is a program that was put on the computer to monitor keystrokes. And it wasn't put on by the company to watch what its employee is doing, it was loaded by an outside computer that used the same backdoor I did to get into the system."

"Holy shit, how did you find that?" Keg asked and leaned in to get a better look.

"There is always a footprint left behind, but they can be erased if the hacker knows how to backtrack their movements. Whoever did this is good. They still have a lot to learn but, truthfully, most people wouldn't notice the footprint because face it, the average person who works on a computer for their job, they don't know enough to be able to search for small blips in their computers. Computers have programs that work in the background at all times. How do you think the majority of identities are stolen? They aren't following people through stores to steal their purses or wallets, not when they can sit at a computer, hack in, and wait for whoever to do their online banking or shop online and use their credit cards."

"I'm never doing personal shit on my computer again," Crank said and shook his head in disgust. "So, is whoever placed that program stealing personal shit off the clerk's computer?"

"No, they are watching what the clerk is typing, whether email, invoices. Pretty much everything. Whoever it is would know if the clerk paid a bill, or whatever, just as if they sat with them at the computer and watched.

"And here is the woman from the school." Tram hit a button, and a driver's license pic came up. "I know no one got a good look, but this is her because I ran the car tag, which came back to Jerry Rivers. Jerry Rivers married Kadija Suri eighteen months ago. She has been the shipping clerk for a year, moving from the receptionist to replace the lady who retired from that position." The screen changed, and the kid from the high school picture popped up.

"This is JJ. The nickname is short for Jerry Junior."

"Excellent fucking work, Tram. Now to figure out what they are up to and how they are connected to each other. Patel's going to need to be brought up to date. After the last two men are caught, brothers, we can head home." I patted Tram on the shoulder.

"I can get on board with that," Moose said, and the others nodded in agreement.

"I'm going to stay logged into the computer at the carrier place. I want to see if I can tap into that keystroke program. If I can, we will be able to watch Kadija work, too," Tram said as he continued to work on the computer.

"Tomorrow morning then, let's hit this shit early and see what we can find out." Everyone agreed except Tram who was already in the zone and ignoring us.

I walked out of Tram's room with the others after we set our agenda for the next day. On the way to my room, I

135

stopped at the vending machines, then with a Coke in hand, I unlocked my door and entered the quiet room.

Replaying everything from the day in my mind, because I felt I was missing something, but what, I couldn't pinpoint. I stripped and laid down on the bed. If I was going to get any sleep, I was going to have to clear my head. I knew exactly what to do to obtain that. I had grabbed my cell on the nightstand and scrolled my contacts until I found the one I wanted and pushed the button.

"Kaden?"

"Hey, Red," I said, my voice hinted with a little of the tiredness I felt in my body.

"Is something wrong, Kaden?"

"Nah, just tired. I wanted to check on you, though before I crashed."

"Oh. I'm fine. Still haven't heard from Roach, but nothing I can do about that other than wait. The next move is his. He either takes it, or he doesn't. I know you can't tell me what you are doing, but is it going okay?" When she talked of Roach, I could hear the hurt in her voice even though she tried to cover it up, which made me want to fly back just to smack some sense into the man.

"It's going well. Hope to have it wrapped up in the next couple days. Things are falling into place."

"Well, that's good then, right?"

"Yeah, it is. Red, if you need anything, call Wild Bill. Okay?"

"Why would I do that?"

"Because I asked you to. I didn't call to argue with you."

Charlie would catch on. Did I think she would go along with everything without input? Not in this lifetime. I was in unchartered waters for the first time in my life. Most men might be apprehensive and take it slow. But I wasn't most men. No, I was going to jump in with both feet.

"Fine." Charlie's immediate agreement was proof enough that she was preoccupied with the Roach situation.

"Good, now tell me what else you've been doing." She needed to take a break from the stuff she was dealing with just like I needed to get away from mine for a few minutes.

Charlie talked, and I listened and laughed at times. She told me about her dinner with Katie. Even sharing the part about Mac, Haven's new prospect. The woman was going to be a handful but in the best of ways. I was happy when she said that Travis and the other brothers had checked in on her. As I listened to her, she reverberated what I had already concluded—badass (at least in how she tried to portray herself)—and a huge heart (the part she tried to hide).

We said goodbye an hour later, and I set my cell on the nightstand, relaxing back on the bed. Talking with Charlie had been just what I needed to clear my head and unwind enough for sleep to take me.

CM Books, LLC

Chapter Eleven

Hawk

"Hell, it looks like we might get this shit wrapped up today. Our part anyway. Patel and his crew can do the cleanup. Fuck, we could be home sometime tonight, and I could be in be bed with my woman's warm body next to me," Moose boasted as he and I sat outside the coffee shop watching JJ Rivers seated at a table with his computer while Pinch and Keg sat a few tables over from him. The pair pretending to read and flip through the motorcycle magazines that were picked up to help them blend in at the shop.

Yeah, 'cause nothing yelled "normal" than two big ass men in jeans and t-shirts with tats peeking out from under the sleeves, sitting in a coffee shop reading and leisurely drinking coffee. They looked as if they should be in one of those picture books that ask you to circle what doesn't belong in this picture.

139

"Thanks to Tram and his computer skills we just might be," I answered Moose.

"Ah, you do appreciate my greatness," came through the earpiece. Tram and Crank were across town with their eyes on the two men who were still in their apartment. The men were expected to be on the move today, and Crank and Tram would tail them. We still had two men in the wind and no information on who or where they were.

"Brother, your modesty never ceases in aahing me," Crank said sarcastically, and Tram laughed.

"I wouldn't go that far. But, brother, you being able to mirror the mirror in that program to see what they had been looking at, is pretty fucking impressive. With your skills, Tram, you could be sitting at a desk in your own corner office at any of the computer corporations or doing some spy shit for the government making some serious green," I said and continued to watch the kid as he typed on his computer.

"I spent enough time inside when I was growing up and suffered from asthma. My dad felt bad and bought me a computer, so I had something to pass my time. By the time I was twelve and had grown out of the asthma, as the doctors like to say, let's just say, my dad questioned his judgment on getting me that computer." Tram chuckled.

"Ha, I've met your dad. He's proud of that shit. I heard him tell Wild Bill that it was worth every dollar he spent on that computer."

140

"VP, that might be true, but next time he comes to town as him about the time the cops came to the house. He wasn't so proud then," Tram said.

"Hawk, Patel is going to text when they pick up the woman, right?" Crank asked.

"Yeah, that was what Wild Bill said. General Patel and his team were just landing when he talked with them. Today is her scheduled off day, so that worked out in our favor. The kid's dad is at work, so he's good, at least until he's informed of everything. Damn, I wouldn't want to be in his shoes. Nothing like being informed that you were just a cover. Anyway, let's hope they find something at the house that will give us info on the two missing players," I said as I watched Pinch stand.

"I hope soon, not sure how much more coffee I can stomach. And Pinch needs to have his bladder checked, the brother's been to the can fifteen times." Keg's voice came through as a whisper, followed by Pinch's "Fuck off" as Moose and I chuckled and watched him head to the back of the shop and into the restroom.

"We're heading your way now, Hawk. A few of Patel's men just showed up at the apartment and waved us off," as Crank was talking our cells went off, signaling a text arriving. I reached for mine and Moose did the same.

"Hot damn! One step closer to that plane ride home," Moose shouted and looked over at me and smiled.

"Crank, Tram, did you get the text?" I asked.

"Yeah, we got it. I read it to Crank because we are already on the move. With the woman at the house and the two men in the apartment picked up means they found out some shit. I just wish they would have given us a hint to what," Tram answered.

"Yeah, Tram, because that is how the government works. Patel will tell us after, just like he always does. Mission complete, then the answers."

"True. We'll be at your location in ten. I'm still linked into the computer at the carrier company, want me to stay hooked up? I think I should. I got a feeling the woman didn't work there just as a cover. The place might be linked to their plan somehow."

"I agree, Tram. People don't do random shit, even terrorists. She took a job at that company for a reason. Just as her marriage to Jerry Rivers. Everything is part of their plan," as Moose finished talking, Crank and Tram pulled into a space beside us. I couldn't have said how long we sat there without speaking until Tram's voice broke the silence.

"What the hell?" I looked over to where Tram was sitting in the vehicle beside us with his window down. His head was bent, which meant he was doing something on the computer in his lap.

"Tram, want to let us know what is going on?" Crank said.

"I think we should go inside the coffee shop and ask the kid. Seems he just changed a urinalysis report from his computer on one of the carrier company's drivers. And it immediately went to the manager's computer, which is the kid's dad. The driver has been pulled from his route for retesting and replaced with another driver. I think the kid knows more than we do at this point." Just the way Tram sounded, told me the kid had impressed him.

"Fuckin' A. Well, we can continue to sit here or go have some coffee and experience firsthand how intelligent this kid really is. His records from the school you pulled this morning showed some pretty high scores on his testing. The kid has a lot of colleges interested in him, too," Moose said, and I nodded in agreement.

"Alright, let's do this and hope Patel doesn't ream our asses." I opened the door and stepped out of the SUV. The others followed suit. When we entered the coffee shop heads turned, and Pinch and Keg were already standing at their table.

"We might want to talk with the kid, then move this little gathering somewhere we don't have a bunch of people around," Crank said and looked around the busy shop.

When we walked toward the kid's table, he looked up, and his eyes went wide. We stopped and pulled out the chairs and sat down. JJ was fixing to stand, but Moose and Keg who were on each side of him, laid a hand on his shoulders to keep him in place. Then they sat in the chairs beside him.

Crank was right, we needed to get out of the coffee shop as soon as possible. Nothing brought unwanted attention like six huge men crammed around a table with a young kid.

"I can move if you guys want to sit here. No problem," the kid looked at each of us as he spoke.

143

"You don't have to move. We actually sat here to talk with you." I watched him swallow, and then his back stiffened and he sat up straight in the chair.

"Kadija's been caught, so there's not going to be anyone to pay your fee after you kill me."

I bent my head so the kid wouldn't see my grin. When I looked back at him, I steeled my features. "What have you been doing on that computer for the last six hours?"

He frowned, then looked down at his computer, then back up at me. "Working on a paper for my English class." I'd give it to the kid, he lied with ease.

"What are you writing your paper on? The art of hacking?" Tram asked, and when the kid didn't answer, he continued. "Your paper won't be accurate because you'll be missing the piece on 'how to cover the footprints'."

The kid stared at Tram, then looked around the table again at each of us. "If you guys don't work for Kadija. Who do you work for?"

I grinned at the kid. "Nice try."

"I wondered if they believed what I sent them. I didn't know since no one got back in contact with me. I mean, I didn't leave my name or anything, but I figured they could find me if they believe the information."

"They did. They tracked you to the school. That's how we found you."

The kid relaxed back in his chair. "Oh, cool. When no one made contact, I thought they didn't take the information I put on that military site seriously. So, I tried to do what I could to halt Kadija and the others' plan." We all nodded. "Am I going to be in a lot of trouble?"

The way he sounded when he asked about getting into trouble was when his true age came out. It'd be easy to forget this kid was still in high school with some of the things he'd accomplished.

"Can't say. But you are going to have to tell everything. Why you did it? How you found out about it? All of it, JJ." When I finished talking, JJ nodded.

"My dad didn't know about her. I tried to tell him, but he thought I made it up because I never hid it from him that I didn't like her. I know he's going to be hurt; I just hope he'll eventually forgive me. He's all I got. My mom died in a car accident twelve years ago. He raised me. It was just him and me. He met Kadija when she started working at the company where my dad works."

"I'm sure he'll be fine. Might take him a bit but he'll get over it." I didn't know what else to tell the kid, and I hoped his dad did what I said. "We got time, so why don't you start at the beginning and tell us everything you know and did."

By the time the kid was finished, I was sure, as I looked around the table, we must have all worn the same expressions. Christ, this kid was smart, inventive, and whatever he decided to do in life, he would make a difference.

"What do you plan on doing after you graduate?" I asked. Curiosity got the best of me.

"I want to be a Navy SEAL." JJ hadn't hesitated in his reply.

"Got no doubt you won't do just that. How about we go to a restaurant? You can call your dad and have him meet us there. We can eat and wait for the General to show up when they're finished. He'll want to ask you some question, JJ, but he will be able to answer some of yours, too. He's the man in charge. Just be honest with him and don't hold nothing back." The kid nodded in agreement.

The kid had ridden the bus to school, but instead of attending, he had walked the coffee shop and been there ever since. We left the shop, and the kid rode with Moose and me.

Once we arrived and got settled at a table big enough to hold us, we waited to order. I had messaged the General and told him where he could find us and that we had the kid and were waiting for the father to arrive. JJ had called him and told him to meet him there and when the dad had asked why, JJ just said there was something he needed to tell him.

We didn't have long to wait before the General walked in and he no more than sat down when Jerry, JJ's dad, arrived.

Introductions were made and when Mr. Rivers was informed of his wife's participation in a terrorist cell, and what all JJ was responsible for, he looked at his son. Even finding out about the betrayal of a woman he thought loved him, I saw the proudness in his eyes for everything his son had accomplished. It told me JJ and his dad would be fine once the dust settled.

146

"Now for all of JJ's computer skills: the changing of the drug test results so you, Mr. Rivers, would pull the driver had to be by far the most ingenious of the things he did. He played a big part in this operation and had no clue he was doing it. If we hadn't gotten the last message on the site that he thought they knew something was up and were following him, we wouldn't be here right now. Their plan would have happened, and the end result wouldn't have been pretty because we hadn't planned to be here for a couple more weeks. His last message expediated our trip.

"I've shared with you JJ's part, and I'm going to tell you what he stopped, but understand I inform you of what they had planned to do with what they would have obtained without your son's interference."

JJ looked disappointed at the General's words but nodded in understanding along with his dad.

"The two that were tasked to follow your son were more or less just muscle for your wife and the other two men. We had trouble locating the last two men and hadn't even known their identity. One of them was an American who was in some financial trouble and they were using him to get the product they were after. He was picked up this morning, and he cracked under the pressure put on him. The last one was the driver you pulled. He was to pick up the product from the lab when he was there to pick up the other items that your company handles for the lab. It was a planned terrorist attack that was stopped with JJ's help," General Patel finished and looked at JJ and his dad and their shocked faces at the magnitude of the situation was brought into the light for them.

"I feel like I am in a movie. This shit is so surreal. I can't imagine Kadija having a part in this. I mean, I believe you. The evidence speaks for itself, but she hid that side of herself very well." Mr. Rivers shook his head in disbelief on how easily he'd been duped.

"They do, Mr. Rivers. You aren't the first civilian used; you surely won't be the last. They move into communities, build trust with the people around them, which allows them to move freely and blend in," I said, and Mr. Rivers nodded.

"JJ, before I forget. I heard," the General looked at me, then back at the kid, "you want to be a Navy SEAL?" JJ looked at me while he nodded. "Well, son, we would love to have you in the military that's for sure. I'll be glad to help in any way you need me to. I've already put in a call to the commander at the Naval Academy. They'll going to contact your school for a copy of your test scores and then your final transcripts once you graduate, but from what Hawk and others said about your grades and scores, that is just a technicality. So expect to hear from them. And don't be shocked if the other branches don't flood you with mail. You possess skills that would make any branch happy to have you in their ranks."

The expression on JJ's face was priceless. Nothing was better than having what could have been a devastating situation turn into one where we came out on top and helped a kid to start on a journey I had no doubt would lead to an impressive future.

As we ate, JJ asked questions about the military and what MOSs we thought were the best in each branch. It shouldn't have surprised any of us that the kid knew more information on the branches' specialties than most soldiers who have been in the service for years. Tram smirked at a few of JJ's statements and I wondered if the same thought ran through Tram's mind—the hope that JJ hadn't gotten some of his information by hacking into the military's databases.

Mr. Rivers relaxed more as the conversation flowed and the realization that his son, though doing illegal things himself, had kept him and his father safe. None of us mentioned that if the terrorists had succeeded, they would have gotten rid of anything and anyone who could have fingered them.

We finished dinner and goodbyes were said, and I and the others went back to our motel. Before the General had left, he handed over the file that shared everything he hadn't been able to talk about with JJ and his dad around.

"Damn, this report is wild. Do you know how many could have died if they had succeeded in replacing the liquid agent the military was going to use in a joint training exercise that was also to be witnessed by a few visiting dignitaries? The military instead of using a non-live agent, they would have been using pure lectin that had been pulled from the seeds of castor oil plants. Christ, there isn't an antidote for that yet. Depending on how much of the shit is ingested in

149

your system, plus how strong or weak your system is, determines if you can survive the symptoms," Moose read the report to us as we stood in my room.

"Brothers, we caught a break on this shit." Everyone was in agreement.

"Sometimes, it is just luck," Crank said.

"With this outcome, I'll take luck anytime," Keg replied.

"I have to agree with that. So now that luck helped in wrapping our job up earlier than we planned, do we head out tonight or in the morning?" I didn't want to stay another night. I wanted to get back, but I would leave it up to them.

"I vote tonight," Keg was the first to answer.

"Tonight. I want to sleep in my own damn bed," Pinch said.

"You know what I want to do." Moose cocked his brow. Yeah, I knew exactly what he wanted, to be with Katie. Charlie was on my mind, too.

Crank and Tram beat me in agreeing that we head out tonight. "Well, it looks as if we are heading home. Let's get packed and ready to roll. I'll text the General and tell him we'll leave the stuff we borrowed in the rooms and the bikes parked out front. He'll send a team over to collect them. We can turn the SUVs in at the airport. Meet in say, fifteen?" The others nodded and headed out of my room to their own.

We were loaded into the vehicles and headed to the airport in under ten. If that didn't show we were ready to get back to Haven, nothing would.

At the airport, I pulled out my phone and texted Charlie that I was headed back, and it would be late when I got in. Her reply that her day just got better surprised and pleased me. Then she texted that Roach had finally come by. I grinned at the text. The old man had wised up, I was glad. The next text held the password to her keyless garage door opener. I hit the thumbs up emoji, then shut my phone down and headed to the plane. Hoping there'd be no delay with the flight.

CM Books, LLC

Chapter Twelve

Charlie

Katie stopped by before her shift to check on me and had just left when the doorbell rang. I sat the book down that I'd picked up to read and walked to the door and swung it open, thinking maybe Katie had forgotten something.

"I know you weren't expecting me, but I figured if I called you might not let me come over." Roach stood on my stoop with an album in his arms.

"Finally decide to come to see me, did you? Heaven forbid you could have spoken to me the other day instead of taking off." I knew I wasn't being fair and didn't care at the moment. I'd wondered for the last couple of days if he was ever going to call or make an appearance.

Roach looked down at me and nodded. "Fair enough. I didn't leave because I found out I had a granddaughter and a son. I left, Charlie, to grieve for a woman I once loved more than my own life and then to come to terms that the same woman kept you both from me. Can you understand that?"

I opened the door wide and waved him in. Once we were in my living room and seated, I answered, "Yes, because my dad and I felt the same way. I not sure I even understand how she lived with herself for not telling him or me about you sooner."

"I should have left with her, Charlie. She left here because she wasn't happy with the direction the club was going, but I couldn't leave Haven to crumble under that shithead Stone. Haven has always been a part of my life; Annie knew that when we got together. I prospected under Wild Bill's grandad, then Wild Bill's old man took over and I backed him. Never liked Stone. To me, he'd always been sneaky and up to no good. But I couldn't catch that bastard doing anything wrong, but I felt it deep in my gut. Geez, I was a dumbass. I hadn't officially put a cut on her to make her my ol' lady, and I hadn't placed a ring on her finger either. Pride got the best of me when she so easily left that I never searched for her.

"Charlie, my angriness for not being told I had a son or hell, a note after she moved to tell me she was pregnant. She'd didn't have to want me, Charlie, for me to do good by my boy. I feel cheated out of watching him grow up and you. I needed a little time to move past that, but I realized that while I was licking my wounds, I was also wasting more time getting to know my granddaughter."

What he said and the sadness in his voice tore at me. I didn't want to be mad or hurt. I wanted to get to know my grandfather.

"When my grandmother spoke those few words about you after her stroke, a stroke they said cost her a lot of her memories, and even trying to remember the smallest of things would be a struggle for her. They were right. She couldn't remember the important things about you, like your name or anything that would have made finding you a piece of cake, but she was able to pull parts of you out and she tried to share them. So, I would like to think you were important enough to her, that pieces of you stuck and not even a stroke could take you completely away from her." Roach's eyes were glassy after I was done, and so were mine.

"I brought a photo album that Annie filled when we were together. I thought maybe you would like to see her how I saw her."

I nodded because I couldn't talk for the lump that had formed in my throat. But I did get up and go to my bookshelf and I pulled down an album of my own. When I sat on the couch, Roach scooted so he sat next to me.

"I would love to look at the pictures of her and you together. And here is one that holds different pictures of my dad and me. Thought you might like to see some of him."

"Tell me about him, Charlie. What's his name? And what does he do for a living?"

"His name is Sean. Sean Spencer Rhoades to be exact." Roach wiped at his eyes as I continued, "And he actually just got a promotion. He made Captain. He is a cop with the Chicago PD."

"My son's a cop?" The way he said cop made me want to laugh.

"Yep."

"Well hell, they always say Karma will come back at you. Bet that bitch is having a good laugh. My son's a cop, and my granddaughter's a bounty hunter." I couldn't help it, I laughed because he sounded so wounded.

He smiled at me and we sat back on the couch and flipped through the albums. Roach talked about his time in the military and with Haven. And I shared growing up in Chicago, small things about my grandmother, my mom, and of course everything I could think of about my dad.

"Dad and Mom are coming here in a few weeks. He wants to meet you."

"What were you going to do if I didn't want to meet him or get to know you?"

"Please, I knew you would show up. Eventually. Besides, I already decided today that you were only getting a couple more days to yourself. Come Monday, you were going to see me whether you wanted a relationship or not. But how could you not want to get to know me? I'm awesome." I chuckled, and Roach shook his head.

"Modest, too."

I looked at the clock. We had been talking and getting to know each other longer than I thought. It was past time for dinner.

"You hungry, Gramps?" The look on his face made me chuckle. "Too soon?"

"Umm... I'm not sure it is ever going to be time for you call me 'Gramps.'"

"Come on, Roach, you can talk to me while I fix us something to eat. I'm hungry."

While we ate the sandwiches I made, a text pinged on my phone. When I looked at it, I smiled and replied.

"Time for me to go. Only a man can put that look on a woman's face and I sure ain't ready for that shit." Roach stood, and he and I walked to the door.

"It was Kaden. They're heading back."

"Good, and that is all I want to know."

I couldn't help but smile. He may not recognize it, but he was already acting like a grandfather.

"Ah come on, I thought you'd want to know *everything* about me."

He opened the door and stepped out. "You are a smartass, aren't you? I bet you gave your dad hell?"

"You bet I did, Gramps." I leaned in and kissed his cheek, closing the door in his face before the shock wore off it.

"My son is a cop and he raised a fucking troublemaker. Fucking great," Roach said, but I could hear the humor in his voice.

When I heard a bike start, I walked back to my living and sat down, picking up the album he had left behind. I flipped to the first picture again and smiled. It was my grandmother and Roach, about the same age as Kaden and I

157

now, sitting on a motorcycle. Someone had to have taken the shot and caught them at the perfect moment. Roach's head was turned and my grandmother was kissing him on the cheek.

The more pages I flipped of the album, the closer I felt to both of them. When I was done, I locked up and headed to bed. Since Kaden hadn't acknowledged the last text I sent, I could only hope it went through.

Hawk

My neck hurt and butt was dragging. We should have stayed the night and gotten up in the morning to fly home. Taylor and Latch picked us up at the airport and dropped us each off at our places. I could have been the nice guy and stayed at my place since it was really late but fuck it, I wanted to see Charlie, so I threw my stuff in the bedroom and grabbed the keys to my bike. Five minutes max and like Moose, I was going to have a warm woman beside me.

After I got off my bike and used the outside keypad to the garage, I rolled the bike in, closed the door, and walked into Charlie's place. Resetting the alarm and doing a quick check on the back and front doors, I headed up the stairs.

When I entered her room, I stood at the door and just looked at her. She was a sight for my sore eyes and dragging ass. It didn't take me long to strip down, then go in the bathroom and hit the shower. The hot water felt great, and any tension my body might have held, washed away with the grime from traveling.

158

Naked and tired, I slid into the bed and pulled Charlie to me. She felt soft and warm, and I wanted to wake her up and enjoy her body, my cock agreeing as it hardened. But the peaceful look on her face kept me from waking her. She sighed and snuggled closer, and I closed my eyes intending to catch a few hours of sleep before I woke her. It was the only thought I had as I drifted off.

Instead of me waking her, my eyes popped open and looked down my body to find her between my legs with her head bent over my cock. I reached out and wrapped my hand around the red mass of hair and moved it out of the way to watch Charlie's tongue as it licked the underside of my cock. When she reached the top, she swirled her tongue around it, then moved her mouth over the mushroomed head and sucked. At that point my eyes crossed.

Charlie had one hand wrapped around the base while her other hand massaged my balls. As her fingernail raked the sensitive spot under my sac, my hips shot off the bed. With one hand in her hair, I grabbed the bedding with the other and gritted my teeth to hold off the urge to thrust into her mouth, leaving her to work me at her own pace.

Charlie scooted up to put herself in a better position to take more of me into her mouth. Her eyes watched me as she slid my cock over her lips and into her mouth. She took as much of me as she could, then pulled back and did it again. She pumped the remaining part of my cock with her hand as she worked me with her mouth. When she took me to the back of her throat and swallowed, I bent my head back and arched my back, clasping my hand into a fist with the sheet balled up inside it.

"Red, you better not stop," I gritted out as I felt the tingle start in my balls. When Charlie hummed around my cock that was all it took and my balls drew up, leaving me unable to hold off any longer. The grip on her hair tightened, keeping her in place until Charlie relinquished control to me. She relaxed her jaw but kept her hand wrapped around my cock to keep me from shoving deep into her throat and choking her.

I pushed in and then pulled out, leaving only the head to rest between her lips. I wasn't going to last much longer, her mouth was warm and wet, and each time I touched the back of her throat, and she swallowed, it pulled me that much closer. I pumped in and out until even gritting my teeth wouldn't hold the orgasm off any longer. My body shook, my cock pulsed, and my cum filled her mouth. She swallowed every drop, then eased my cock out of her mouth until only the tip remained as she swirled her tongue, lapping the last of my cum before releasing all of me. I relaxed my hips back on the bed and released her hair and the sheet from my grip.

"Fuck, Red, your mouth is lethal. Now come here. I didn't have any dinner, and I'm hungry," I said, and Charlie made her way up my body. She straddled my hips and her hands moved over my chest, stopping only to scrape her fingernails over my nipples.

I reached and grabbed her under the arms until she knelt over my face. "Hold that headboard, Red." Once she

160

had a good hold, I held onto her hips, pulled her closer to my face, and ran my tongue through her folds until I hit her clit, stopping to flick it, then starting over.

"Don't tease me, Kaden." She tried to move her hips to follow my tongue as I held her tight. When she realized I'd stopped licking, she ceased all movement.

"That didn't take you long to figure out," I said, then sucked her clit and bit down gently, giving her no time to answer as she threw her head back and screamed. I eased up on her swollen nub and ran my tongue through her folds, then pushed the tip into her.

Charlie moved one hand down to her clit, and I removed my tongue and stopped again.

"You're an asshole!" she yelled in frustration. I let go of her hip, and the sound of my hand smacking her ass echoed in the room.

"How bad you wanna get off, Red?"

She huffed. "Forget it. Let me go, and I will finish myself off." She tried to move and I slapped her ass again.

"Oh no, you don't. I'll get you off, but it's because my dick's hard again and I want that pussy wrapped around me."

"You are a bastard, and I don't care if I get off now."

"Liar," I said and pierced her pussy with my tongue and began to fuck her until her body started to tremble under my hands, and I knew she was close when her hips moved to chase my tongue. I moved my mouth away and asked again, "How bad do you want to come, Red?"

"Goddammit, Kaden. Make me come!"

161

I grabbed her hips and tossed her down on the bed, flipped her until she laid on her stomach, then I lifted her to her knees and with one hand on her back to hold her shoulders to the bed, I drove my cock into her pussy until she'd taken all of me, sending her over the edge. The angle had me deep, and I piston into her until she bent her head forward and bowed her back, screaming as her body shook from her orgasm. I continued to pump into her as she rode it out. When she went to sag into the mattress, spent, I wrapped one arm around her waist and held her hips up while I bent my body over hers and placed the palm of my other hand on the mattress to keep us both up.

"I don't think I can take anymore."

"Sure you can. I was going to let you sleep, but you woke me up instead. You owe me. Come on, one more, Red. I'll keep fucking you until I get it." I thrust in and out, speeding up my pace. When I felt my own release close, I slid my hand down until I reached her pussy, then I splayed my hand and used my thumb and finger to pinch her clit, sending her over the edge. Her pussy clamped down as I shoved deep one last time and she pulled me over the edge with her.

Charlie fell to the mattress with me behind her, shifting us to the side at the last second to keep from landing on top of her.

"Welcome home," came out muffled and was followed by a tired sigh. When I slid out of her, I realized what I'd done.

162

"Shit, Red. I forgot the condom." When there was no response, I rubbed my hand over my face. "I promise, I'm clean, Red," I said and ran my hand down her back. She mumbled and I couldn't make out what she said. "Can you repeat that?"

"S'k, on the pill."

I never forgot condoms, ever! The feeling of her wrapped around me bare should have been enough to bring me to my senses; no, instead it took what little of control I had. I sighed and I got up and went to the bathroom and cleaned myself up, then came out with a washcloth to do the same for her. After tossing the cloth in the sink, I joined Charlie back in the bed. Pulling her close and closing my eyes, I let Charlie's breathing take me under.

And instead of waking as if I had a nightmare when the vision of a little girl with flaming red hair stood in front of me with her arms raised—I smiled, picked her up and kiss her forehead, accepting the dream as a look of what my future could be with the woman currently in my arms.

CM Books, LLC

Chapter Thirteen

Charlie

We rode into the lot at Haven, and Kaden pulled up to an open spot. I let go of his waist and slid off, standing to the side while he backed it into the space. I looked around the parking lot while I waited for him to cut the engine and dismount. People were still pulling in, and I watched a car park and the doors open. Four women got out, and I looked down at my t-shirt and jeans, then back to them. Shit, I had more material covering my body than they had put together.

"Ready?" Kaden's voice drew me away from the women that were walking across the lot. He put his arm around my shoulder and pulled me in close. I felt his lips touch the top of my head and I looked up at him.

"You know there's a soft side buried under your toughness."

"Only for you, Red." He leaned down and kissed my lips.

I learned a lot about Kaden in the last couple of days. And I'd shared parts about myself with him. I told him about my grandmother and her death. My dad and my mom, and everything leading up to me moving here.

We found in a way that our lives were a little similar. He'd grown up in Washington. His father and mother had owned a horse ranch until they died in a plane crash going to a thoroughbred auction. Kaden owned the farm now, but there weren't any horses on the land. The house on the property was huge but old, and he had it recently renovated. That was why he lived in the same neighborhood I did; it was going to take time to remodel. He had no siblings, just a grandfather who still worked his own farm daily and lived over an hour away. Other than the club, his grandfather was his only family.

After Kaden had done a short stint in the military, he'd rode around the US until he made his way back to Washington, then he joined Haven shortly after he met Wild Bill at the Roadhouse when he'd stopped there to eat.

"What has your eyebrows drawn together?" Kaden asked as we approached the door leading into the clubhouse.

"I was just thinking of all the stuff we talked over the last few days. You know what you didn't tell me?"

"No. What?"

"You lived in the house after you returned from the military. Are you remodeling to sell it?"

"I'm not selling, Red. I just hadn't wanted to live in it with all the updating going on. They finished up right before I left town. The only thing left is to notify my landlord so he

166

knows I'm moving out. Then I only got to move my shit back to the house." Kaden moved his arm from around me and reached for the door.

"Hawk, I was hoping you would be here tonight." I knew the voice had to belong to one of the women who had gotten out the car just a few minutes ago. I turned and verified my own suspicion.

Kaden turned toward the woman who spoke. The brunette was tall with curves that went on forever, and her breasts were big and barely contained in the tank top that looked two sizes too small.

"How's it going, Sarah Jane?" The woman looked at me, then back to Hawk.

"I haven't been able to make it here for a couple months, but I was free and able to make it work tonight. Glad to see you're here. It's been a long time." As Sarah Jane talked, she moved until she stood in front of Kaden with her back to me.

"Yeah, been awhile." The other women stood to the side and listened. Kaden reached around the woman and grabbed my hand and tugged. I moved from behind her and stood beside him. The move didn't even give the woman pause.

"Maybe we can hook up later." She stepped closer to Kaden and ran a red painted fingernail down the middle of his t-shirt and stopped when the finger encountered his belt.

I'd never been the jealous type, but I'd seen enough. "Excuse me," I said and waited for the woman to acknowledge me. She didn't move the finger that rested on his belt, but her eyes cut in my direction and ran up and down as she assessed me.

"Why don't you run along inside, honey, and give Hawk and me a minute. We are old friends who need to get…reacquainted." The other women snickered. People always underestimate me. It's what made me a great bounty hunter.

"Sarah, enough," Kaden's voice held a warning, but evidently it was missed by the woman.

"It's okay, Hawk, I didn't expect for you to go without when I wasn't available. But now that I'm here, you can cut the little one loose. I'm sure there is someone who likes their women on the small side."

"Knock it off, Sarah, or you and your little group can leave."

She looked at Kaden with puppy dog eyes, and I wanted to laugh because the ability to pull off innocence had left her a long time ago. It was time to put a stop to it before we drew a crowd.

"It's okay, Hawk, I knew you had women before me." Sarah couldn't hold the wounded puppy look. When I started to use her wording from before, it didn't take long for her façade to drop. "You can let them stay because I don't want to be the cause of one of the guys not getting their skank fill or filling their skank. Whichever it is. I'm sure some men don't mind strapping a two by four across their ass, so they don't fall in."

"Why you, bitch. By the look of those bruises on your face, it seems like someone else didn't like your mouth—"

"Now, now." I waved a finger back and forth in front of her face. "Don't turn into a *catty* little skank on top of things. And this," I pointed to my cheek and eye, "happened when I headbutted the last bitch that tried to step into my territory. So you might want to take your hand off him and step back. Then you need to ask someone to explain about personal space because if there is another episode like this while I am around—I'll taser your ass. From what I hear if you set the juice high enough, it'll pop breast implants like a balloon." I looked at her breasts to emphasize what I meant, and the look on her face and her little group's faces was priceless. Then I walked through the open door and called over my shoulder, "Coming, babe."

"Right behind you, Red." I heard the amusement in Kaden's voice and smiled.

My grand entrance was put to a halt when I almost ran over Katie. She and Moose stood with Wild Bill and a couple of the other men. Katie had a worried look on her face while the men all wore wide grins.

"Linc wouldn't let me come out there. The eye and cheek are healing nicely by the way. Even the darkest of the bruising has started to turn lighter. How are you feeling?" Katie asked.

I rolled my eyes. "Still tender to the touch but overall not so bad. I've been taking Tylenol instead of the pain pills, and it seems to be working well enough. Now stop worrying. Isn't this supposed to be a party." I glanced into the room and saw people drinking, dancing, and a couple card games going on.

169

"I want to know if what you said about the taser is true." Tram shrugged at Crank when he hit him in the arm.

I laughed. "Honestly, I have no idea, but it sounded good at the time." Everyone laughed and then laughed harder as Sarah and the others walked past to enter the room, and not one looked my way.

"Come to the kitchen. Tink and Macy are in there, too. We are setting out the snacks buffet style so everyone can just grab something when they want."

"Sure." I started to follow Katie and Moose when an arm wrapped around my waist. I looked up, and Kaden winked at me. "I can go to the kitchen by myself. You don't have to stick with me."

"Maybe I want to. Didn't you refer to me as your territory?" Kaden's lips twitched, and I shook my head.

"Men. Is that all you picked up on from outside? Seriously?"

"No, I got something else watching you in action." Kaden grabbed my hand and placed it on his crotch, and I jerked my hand back.

"For fuck's sake that locked up. If he breaks free someone could lose an eye."

Kaden chuckled, then he leaned down and whispered in my ear, "Did the warm bath help? Or are you still sore?"

Kaden had felt bad when I grimaced getting out of bed that morning and filled the tub up and let me soak while he fixed us something to eat. It had felt so good that I dozed, and he had to wake me when he came up upstairs to tell me the food was ready.

"A little stiff but I think that is more due to my lack of sex for the prior six months, which thanks to you, my dry spell has been broken. Add in your size and well... moving around seems to help. I just need to get used to having regular sex."

"Damn, straight. 'Cause I'm more than sure you'll have a lot."

"You are insatiable," I said as we walked through the doorway to the kitchen.

"Only when it comes to you," he said and kissed the side of my head, something I noticed he often did when we were together, as we walked into the kitchen.

Tink and Macy said hi as they passed us with bowls in their hands and Katie was already at the bar helping Roach place hot wings on a platter. Moose was bent in front of a couple coolers filling them with soda that Crank was handing to him.

"What can I do?" I asked, and Katie and Roach looked up.

"Can you look in the cabinets for a few bowls to put pretzels and nuts in? We thought we would set those out on the bar in the main room," as Katie spoke, Roach kept looking at me. Then he stepped from around the counter. He still seemed a little apprehensive, but he pushed through it and hugged me. I hugged him back and smiled at him when we broke apart.

"That shiner is looking a helluva lot better. So you know, I told Shock and Freak about you being my granddaughter. Now when they see me," Roach looked at Hawk, "your girl is all they ask about."

"Huh? They ask about Charlie?" Kaden asked the man.

"Isn't that what I said, Hawk? Who's the old man here?" I grinned at Roach giving Kaden a hard time and then he turned back to me. "Those two don't normally say more than ten words when anyone talks to them. It's nice to see them interested in others enough to carry on a conversation even if it's only checking on you and Katie. Hawk, you and Moose might want to watch your women around those two. Could be they are interested in stealing them away."

Moose grunted, and Katie chuckled as Roach winked at me, then went back to the counter and began filling another platter with wings. I looked up at Kaden to see if he noticed Roach's slip about me being his girl and caught him staring at me.

"What?"

"Checking to make sure you weren't going to flip at his words," Kaden said.

"Me. I was waiting for you to run. It was just words, Kaden. He didn't mean anything by them."

I walked over and opened and closed cabinets to look for the bowls Katie asked for. I found a few smalls bowls in one of the bottom cabinets and bent and grabbed them. When I stood, Kaden was right beside me.

"There's more here," Kaden moved his hand between us, "than just words, Red. I don't flip out or run over something that is true."

"Can we enjoy this between us and see where it leads before we start analyzing it?" I asked and waited for his reply.

"Not sure, I can." He turned and walked over to where Moose was and started helping load the coolers.

CM Books, LLC

Chapter Fourteen

Hawk

"Charlie fits in well with the other women." Moose and I sat at the bar drinking a beer and watching the women who sat at a nearby table playing cards and laughing.

"Yeah, she does." I watched Charlie throw her head back as she laughed at something Tink said and smiled.

"So, what's the deal, brother? Seems you jumped in with both feet." Moose tilted his head toward the table the women sat at, then finished the beer he was nursing and sat the bottle on the bar.

"What's that supposed to mean?"

"Damn, don't get worked up. Just saying that you two walked in here pretty damn comfortable with each other. I also noticed she didn't ride her own bike but was rode bitch with you." Moose cocked his brow.

"You got an ol' lady, Moose. Why you worried about Charlie?" I glared at him, and he grinned.

"Not her I'm worried about, brother. I'm worried for the man who once told me *'Grab her and kiss the hell out of her.'* Do you remember what I told you when you said that?"

I frowned and tried to remember the conversation he referred to but came up blank.

"I can tell by the expression on your face you don't remember. Let me remind how that played out. It was when I had eyes on Katie and I took over for Taylor, and you decided to keep me company. Your advice on how to get her back was and I quote, *'You could always try walking up to the door and ringing the bell. When she answers the door kiss the hell out of her.'* Taylor laughed and got the hell out of there so fast that I'm surprised Katie and Charlie hadn't heard the squeal of his tires."

Moose was smiling and enjoying himself a little too much. The asshole. "Fuck you. You were the one whining about the girl you let go. I was just sick of hearing that shit from a grown ass man."

"Bullshit, watching you fall, Hawk, has been the highlight the last few weeks. What I told you that day has already started and you, my friend, are way past going back to your glorified single days."

"Well, what the fuck did you say to me?" I sneered.

"That a woman was going to walk up and bring Kaden Cross to his knees." Moose did a chin lift, then continued, "And, brother, here comes the one who has."

I looked away from him and watched as Katie and Charlie walked toward us. "You don't know what you're talking about." I refused to tell the asshole he was right. And Moose's reply was to burst out laughing.

"What so funny?" Katie asked as she walked and stood beside Moose.

"Just reminding Hawk of a conversation he and I had that was amusing." The humor could still be heard in Moose's voice.

"Maybe you should share it so we can laugh, too," Charlie said and moved in between my legs and then leaned into me and planted a kiss on my chin.

"Nah, I don't think you women would appreciate the humor." Moose looked at me and smirked. For a second I wondered how upset Wild Bill would be if I killed Haven's Sergeant at Arms.

"You enjoying yourself, Red?" Charlie at me and smiled.

"I would enjoy myself more if you would dance with me. That's why Katie and I came over here."

"Is that so?"

"Yep, we want to see if you boys move as smooth on the dance floor as you do in other places." Moose chuckled at Charlie's words, Katie blushed, and Pinch groaned as he walked behind the bar.

"See what happens when ol' ladies are around. Way too much information gets thrown out there, and we hear shit about our brothers that we should never have to hear. 'Cause fuck, you can't undo it, and then every time you see them that shit pops into your mind. Like now, Tink and Macy's conversation about Smoke and Fire is in there."

177

Pinch shifted the bottles of beer he'd grabbed and held them by the neck of the bottles with one hand so he could point to his temple with his free hand. "'Cause whatever the ears hear, the brain puts pictures to it. To hell with beer," Pinch reached under the bar and pulled out a bottle of Jameson, "this is what I'm going to need. Shit around here gets stranger by the day."

I looked at Charlie, then over at Katie, and when I looked at Moose, he shook his head. We knew why the women just stared at Pinch. It was probably the first time they'd heard him say so much at one time. Out of all of us, he was the quietest, but if he got riled up, it was on and usually funnier than shit.

"What's stranger? The fact there hasn't been a fight break out or someone tweaking in the corner. Maybe you are missing the guns being drawn during the card games because someone was accused of cheating," Moose brought up some of the crap that happened regularly when we first joined Haven, and Stone and his following were at the parties.

"Freak and Shock came out of the basement a bit ago and sat down with Prez, Keg, Crank, Tram, Roach, and me. I came out to get everyone something to drink."

"Did they say if something was wrong?" I asked.

"Nope, they said they would have been up earlier, but Jasmine was acting strangely. Then they asked if Katie and Charlie were still here. See, it all comes back to ol' ladies. I'm putting this out here right now, I'm never taking an ol' lady. The day I do will be the day I let Crank close to Madison. And you know that shit will never happen."

"Madison is your sister, right?" Katie asked.

"Yes."

"You don't want her with a biker? You're a biker," Charlie asked and waited for Pinch to answer.

"I got no problem with her being with a biker. Just not Crank, he's my best friend, and no way do I want to know he is doing my baby sister."

"Umm... I'm confused. Wouldn't you want her with your best friend? I mean, you know him. Plus you know he would treat her good," Katie asked, and Moose and I both groaned.

"No, my sister is innocent and Crank, well... let's just say he is into things she wouldn't understand."

"Dude, how old is your sister?" Charlie asked.

"Not old enough for Crank." Since Pinch wasn't going to answer her, I would. I didn't want her to think that any of the men went for underage girls. Haven already had dealt with that shit.

"Madison is out of college and works at the bank, Charlie," I said, and Charlie rolled her eyes.

"You do realize that she has probably already done the nas—"

Pinch cut Charlie off as he came around the bar with the liquor bottle in one hand and the beers in the other. "Nuh uh, don't want to hear that, because then the images come. Did you not hear me before? Some things stay with you. Madison is my sister, and I do not want the visuals of her and any man."

Pinch walked off, and Charlie looked up at me. "Is he serious?"

"As a mother fucking heart attack," Moose said and stood. "Come on, sweetheart, I'll dance with you." He pulled Katie to the floor.

"I guess you expect me to dance with you, too?" I asked.

"Well, it's up to you. If you don't want to hold me tight and let our bodies rub together, there's nothing I can do about it."

I moved her back as I stood. "Dancing is like having sex, Red, so remember there is a room full of people who will hear if you moan."

Charlie's mouth dropped opened, and I pulled her to the dance floor. My dick was already hardening with the thought of her tight little body pressed against mine.

180

Chapter Fifteen

Charlie

Good God, I didn't think there was anything the man did poorly. Kaden Cross needed to come with some type of warning stamped on his forehead for women to see. I laid my head against his chest, and he bent and rested his chin on top of my head. I sighed and closed my eyes and enjoyed how it felt to be held tight in his arms.

"What was that sigh for, Red?"

"You'll think I'm crazy." I could've lied and just said I was tired, but I didn't play games. Never had.

"Try me. I'm not easily spooked."

"I feel comfortable around you as if I've known you longer than a few weeks. And I know it's crazy because we really don't know each other."

"Red, I thought you wanted to let it just be and analyze later?"

"See, I told you it was crazy." Kaden chuckled and squeezed me. "Glad my crazy makes you laugh." I tried to move out of his arms, but he wouldn't release me.

"Stop it. I'm sorry, I laughed because whatever this is between us scares you. A woman who tackles men and tracks down criminals who try to run."

"I didn't tackle Wyan, we ran into each other. You could at lea—"

"Can you let me finish, or do you want to argue?"

"Fine. Continue." I laid my head against his chest again as he kept us swaying with the music.

"We do know each other, Red." I tilted my head back to look up at him.

"Physically."

Kaden stopped dancing, dropped his arms, and stepped back. I couldn't miss the irritated look on his face. He grabbed my elbow and began leading me out of the room and continued until we were in the parking lot.

A few members were off to one side smoking, and Kaden turned us in the opposite direction. When we reached the end of the building, he turned me to face him and stared down at me.

"I know you are a strong woman, who likes to be in control of her life, but who is still able to trust enough to turn over the reins. A woman who goes for what she wants and doesn't care what others think about it. You're able to look past a person's exterior to what makes them tick. You moved across the country to find a grandfather you've never met, even though you didn't know if he would be accepting

182

of the gesture or even still living. Family means something to you. You're not only happy with their achievements, but you also celebrate with them. And you never do anything halfway, it is all or nothing, to include love."

No words came, I just stood there and looked up at him.

"How the fuck is that for knowing you, Charlie?" Before I could get anything to come out of my mouth, Kaden turned and walked back inside. I don't know how long I stood there and stared at the spot where he disappeared out of my sight. But I did feel as though he took a piece of me with him.

"He's a good man, honey." I turned and looked at Roach, and he smiled at me. "Not sure what you were arguing about to make him walk off like that, but it can't be that bad."

"We weren't really arguing. Kaden told me a few things he saw in me, and when he was done, I just couldn't find the words to answer."

"Oh. Well, Charlie, we're a hard ass bunch, rough around the edges. We shoot off at the mouth sometimes when we get angry and we don't mean it. I'd volunteer to kick his ass for you, but from what I know about you, you can probably do a better job of it."

I couldn't help it, I laughed. "Roach, it wasn't like that. I mentioned we really didn't know each other and damn if he didn't prove me wrong. He's seen more of me, in the short time he's known me than a few men did who I was with for months."

"I get that. Now, I also heard you were a go get 'em type girl. Don't be like this crusty old man and live each day with regret."

I knew he was talking about not following my grandmother when she left. "She was a special woman, huh?"

Roach's eyes sadden. "Yeah, she was. You remind me so much of her."

I smiled at him. "Hope it is a good thing."

Roach ran his eyes over my face. "Oh yeah. She was a beautiful woman and strong just like you are. Now, are you going to stand out here and talk with me or take care of business?" Roach moved and placed his hand on the small of my back and gave me a little shove.

I stood on my tiptoes and kissed his cheek. "Something else you Haven men have in common—you're all bossy as hell."

Roach's laughter followed me as I headed for the entrance. "We are growing on you, girl!" he yelled as I opened the door.

"Like a fungus!" I yelled over my shoulder as the door closed behind me. He was right, they were growing on me. So much had changed over the last few days. I had a grandfather to get to know and a man it seemed. Well, if he would still have me.

Once inside, I looked around the room and I saw Katie and Moose talking with Freak and Shock, but no Kaden. I walked toward the group and when I approached Freak stood and offered me his seat.

184

"Thanks, Frankie, but you sit. I'm looking for Kaden."

"Anything wrong, Charlie?" Moose asked and frowned. Well, I was glad at that point that Kaden hadn't shared with the whole group.

"Uh no, just lost him."

"When we were coming to say hi to you and Katie, Kaden walked into the kitchen. Your face looks much better today, Charlie," Shock said.

"Thanks, Steven. I'm glad to see you and Frankie here." I smiled at both men, and they smiled back. "You need to come upstairs more often so we can dance together. Bet you guys could teach Katie and me a few things." The pink that rose on their cheeks was cute.

"Don't know why you young girls would want to dance with two old coots for," Frankie said.

"I'm wondering the same thing," Moose mumbled.

"Linc Harris, that isn't nice," Katie pinched him, and he rubbed the spot on his chest.

"Brother's just worried you might realize we were the better men," Steven said and then laughed when Moose glared at him and Frankie.

"I'm going to go find Kaden. You men try to behave yourselves. Better yet, don't." I winked at Frankie and Steven, then told Katie that I would talk with her soon and received the typical chin lift from Moose.

When I walked into the kitchen, Kaden sat at the table, his head bent with his phone in his hand and his thumb sliding on the screen like he was searching. I didn't want to disturb him, so I stood in the doorway and watched

185

him. Kaden really was a good looking man. His sandy blond hair was short, and his eyes were dark green and framed by eyelashes women could only achieve with make-up or fake ones. They were thick, long, and almost brushed his cheeks as he looked down.

A few members and a couple hang-arounds moved around the food that was spread out, and Kaden never noticed them, he was so focused on what he was doing. When he finished with what he was looking at and was putting the phone in his back pocket, I walked up behind him and placed my hands on his shoulders. Kaden didn't look at me, but he did sit up straight as I rubbed his shoulders and down his arms, then back again.

"As a young girl, my mother told me how she and my dad had met, and after a few dates with him, she knew he was the one for her. And she'd been lucky that he had felt the same way. I listened and imagined what having that connection with someone would feel like.

"When I got older and saw the affections they besotted on each other, I knew I would never settle for anything less. Then I started dating and my thinking changed with every relationship I entered until finally, I had stopped looking for or expecting to find anyone to share what they had found together. I pretty much resigned myself to the fact that I would end up like my grandmother, alone because no one would care enough for me.

"I know you are a strong man who goes after what he wants. You're bossy, protective, and you are loyal to Haven and its members. When you enter a room, respect is given,

186

not because you are the VP, but because you have earned it. Family means something to you, too. I noticed that when you talked about your parents and your grandfather. So, we do know each other. And I want to know more." I leaned down and place a kiss on his neck, then rested my chin on his head and draped my arms over his shoulders to where they hung down in front of him. "Because I found that person, Kaden. You."

Kaden didn't say a word. He unhooked my arms and stood, then he turned around and cupped my face in his hands, being careful of my cheek that still showed some bruising.

"The day at Katie's place when you walked over, I wasn't expecting you. Fuck, I wasn't even looking for you. But there you were. You're stuck, Charlie. So, we are gonna do this. We aren't going to analyze shit, and we sure as fuck aren't going to do a shit ton of talking about it. I want you to move in my house with me. I don't want any arguments on the matter, and I sure as shit don't want to hear a fuckin' thing in regards to us not knowing each other. You didn't open the door to come after me, you kicked it in. Now, Red, you're going to have to put up with me."

I had a chance to blink, and that was it. He bent his head and took my mouth with his. Kaden's tongue licked my lips, and I opened them, letting him in. His tongue dominated as he took total possession of my mouth. When he broke the kiss, I was panting and a little dazed. Kaden's forehead rested against mine, and he was the first to recover.

"We'll go to your place tonight, and we are going now." He let go of my face, put his arm around me, and led me toward the door.

On our way out we yelled goodbye to everyone and were on Kaden's bike headed toward my house. It definitely looked as if we were doing this.

We barely made it in the house and got the door closed when he pushed me back against it and started kissing me. Kaden only broke the kiss long enough to pull my shirt over my head, then his lips were back on mine. My bra followed next. My pants were more of an issue, and he had to break the kiss and step back to push them all the way down. My boots were removed so he could relieve me not only of the pants but my thong, too. There was something to be said for being naked while he was completely dressed.

Kaden stood back up, and his face got close to mine until all I could see was his eyes. "Red, you are as close to perfection as a woman can get."

I reached up and ran my fingers through his hair and closed the space between us until our lips met. I started the kiss, but he took over and devoured me. It was the only word to describe his demanding and thoroughly dominating kiss, which left me breathless. Neither of us could get enough of each other. Our tongues dueled, and he ran a hand down my side, reaching my hip. His roughened hands running over my bare skin had goosebumps breaking out.

Kaden's hand slid behind me and grabbed the cheeks of my butt where he squeezed and caressed. When he lifted

188

me up, I wrapped my legs around his waist bringing my bare pussy in contact with the material of his jeans. My clit throbbed when I shifted to gain a better grip with my legs, and it came in contact with his very hardened cock. I rolled my hips, and he groaned and broke the kiss. The desire he held for me had darkened the green in his eyes. His nostrils flared and his arms adjusted until only one held me up while his other hand moved between us to unzip his pants.

Kaden pulled his cock free and it rested between my leg, hard, and I could feel the heat of its touch. He pushed his hips forward and his cock slide through my folds. I squeezed, and he groaned when I tightened on his length.

"Ready, Red?"

"I've been ready, take me," I whispered. I gasped when he dipped his head and bit my nipple then laved it with his tongue.

"Oh God, that feels good." I leaned my head back against the door and just felt.

"You are wet for me?" he whispered against my breast, and I nodded. "So wet, my dick is slick with your cream. I don't know if I what to fuck you or eat you."

Never had I been talked to so bluntly during sex, but I had missed out because the more he said, the wetter I became.

"Why choose?" I panted out as he kissed his way up from my breasts. He bit my earlobe, then swirled his tongue around the outline of my ear.

"Ah, my woman's greedy. I like that. But you're going to have to wait to get my mouth on your cunt because I want to feel that pussy stretched around my cock.

Kaden moved back, his cock sliding through my wetness until the head was at my entrance. And with one thrust of his hips, he pushed into the hilt and my back arched, my shoulder hitting the door. He held still long enough for me to adjust to his size and then he pulled out and thrust in again. Any earlier discomfort from being oversexed was forgotten.

I rolled my hips and flexed, tightening around him. He hands gripped me so hard that I knew I would have bruises, but it would be so worth it for the feeling I was experiencing.

"Tight as a glove and so wet and warm. Your pussy was made for me."

I moaned as Kaden picked up speed. He began to pull me down as he thrust up. As he continued to pound into me, the only things heard in the room were my moans, his groans, and the slapping of my skin against the door.

"I'm so close!"

"Me too. Take us over, Red."

I laid my forehead on his shoulder and reached between us and rubbed my swollen clit, matching the speed of his thrust. I pinched my clit and bit down on his shoulder through his t-shirt as he slammed into me. His cock twitched inside me and he filled me with his cum as my body shook with my own climax.

Minutes went by, or it could have been hours as we stood there. "How was that?" I breathlessly asked.

190

"I came so hard, I saw stars," Kaden answered while he held me up and worked on catching his breath.

"Does that mean you're not going to eat me?"

"Fuck, when you talk all nasty and shit, my dick gets hard."

Kaden didn't lie. I felt his cock growing hard inside me. He kept us connected as he turned away from the door and started walking through the house. When he reached the stairs, he pulled one of my arms loose and moved it down to his waist.

"Hold up my pants while I get us upstairs. I think I'm ready for my midnight snack and I got one for you, too. You can suck my cock why I'm eating you out. And I'll take that twitch of your pussy as a yes?"

Kaden got us up the stairs and into the bedroom. When he pulled out of me, I felt the loss of him as I slid down his body until my feet hit the floor.

"You going to answer?" he asked as he removed his clothes. Damn, his body was prime. "Well?"

"Crap, was I supposed to answer something? Don't ask questions and strip at the same time. I lose my thoughts and can't talk."

"Can't think or talk. Hmm... I'll store that information." He chuckled at my frown.

"You want to talk? You promised me a meal." I laughed when his cock twitched. Then my body was in the air until it hit the bed and bounced.

Kaden walked over and laid down and pulled me on top of him. "Flip around, time to eat."

191

Who was I to argue? I was a little hungry.

CM Books, LLC

Chapter Sixteen

Hawk

"Damn, they did a great job on the renovation. I need to find one of these old farmhouses for myself and fix it up," Keg said and set the box down in the living room.

"What would you do with a place this big? We've been to your apartment. You're a slob, brother." Crank sat the box he was carrying down beside Keg's.

"Less talking and more lifting." I walked into the living room holding one end of Charlie's TV while Moose held the other. We set it down on the stand Tram, and Pinch had carried in earlier.

"You know it is sad when your woman has a bigger TV than you do." Keg laughed and walked over to take a better look.

"Yeah, but Kaden has the bigger entertainment device that I like." I smiled as Charlie walked in and looked around.

"I don't need to hear that my granddaughter likes Kaden's big device!" Roach yelled from the kitchen, and we all laughed.

"Stop laughing. You could have warned me he was in there," Charlie whispered and walked toward me. I leaned down and planted a kiss on her lips.

"What fun would there be in that?" I asked as I walked past her. The others continued to laugh.

"Assholes, every fucking one of you," she mumbled, then yelled, "Sorry, Gramps!"

"It's still too early for that!" Roach yelled back, and I looked over at Charlie, who smiled like she always did when she and Roach did that.

"Here's the last of it. Where you want it, honey?" Freak asked as he and Shock carried in the coffee table. Charlie moved the box that sat in front of the couch and then motioned for the two to put it there.

I shook my head when she kissed each one on the cheek and told them thanks for helping her get moved in. I wasn't the only one who watched the interaction between the three. When I looked over at Moose, he shrugged. Not one of us could explain the change in Shock and Freak since Katie and Charlie had become a part of Haven. We weren't going to question it either, we were just going to go with it. Life was easier that way.

"Thanks, brothers, for helping get mine and Charlie's stuff moved in."

"No thanks needed. Glad to help out," Crank said, and the others nodded.

Roach walked out of the kitchen and stood beside the others. "You men ready to go? Let's leave these two to get Charlie's things put away." Roach put his arm around Charlie.

"More like christen the place," Keg said.

"Keg, you are never going to get a good woman," Roach said and hugged Charlie.

"I don't want a good woman. I want a very, very bad woman." Everyone groaned at Keg's words, even Shock and Freak.

"That would be our cue to leave," Moose said and started for the door, the others following. Each man told Charlie bye as they passed her.

"Gonna walk them out and I will be right back."

"Okay, I'm going to open this box because I think the remote to the TV is in it." Charlie bent down in front of the box, and I walked out to see my brothers off.

After a couple of minutes, I was back in the house, but Charlie wasn't where I left her. I moved through the house and checked the rooms on the first floor, but no Charlie, so I headed up the stairs. When I reached the master bedroom, the door was barely cracked and I pushed it open. What I saw left me speechless.

Charlie laid in the middle of the bed propped up on pillows with not one piece of clothing on and her hand between her spread legs running a finger through her folds, only to stop and circle her clit.

Fuck me, I was only gone a couple minutes, and I could already see the glistening of her pussy. She was wet and ready, and my dick showed his pleasure by instantly becoming hard. As I started to move forward, I began removing my clothes. The t-shirt went first and Charlie watched my hands as I moved them to the button on my jeans. The desire showed in her eyes the closer I got to the bed. When I reached the bed, my pants laid open, and since I hadn't bothered with underwear, my cock sprang free from its confines and bobbed in front of her, her eyes following its movement.

"I'm assuming we aren't unpacking your things today?"

Charlie's eyes snapped up to meet mine and she smiled. "I was going to start but..." She moved her other hand to her breasts and circled each nipple. "I like Keg's idea better."

"You sure you aren't going to bitch when we are done, and none of the stuff is unboxed. Your parents are coming in tomorrow afternoon, remember?"

"Oh, I remember. It also means that we would have to wait to christen any room other than the bedroom why they're here. Not thinking my dad would appreciate walking in to find his little girl laid out like a buffet on the kitchen table. Besides, my mom will help me. She will even think it's fun."

"Okay, but you are in the bedroom now. Why?" As I waited for her to answer, I sat on the bed to remove my boots and pull my pants off. When I turned to look why she hadn't answered, her eyes were shut and her finger was pumping in and out of her pussy. "Oh no, you don't, Red." I

196

grabbed her hand, and as I looked into her opened eyes, I stuck her finger in my mouth and sucked her essence off.

When Charlie went to rise, I shifted, pushed her back onto the pillows and rolled until I was on top of her with the weight of my body resting on my elbows.

"You haven't answered me."

Charlie's green eyes looked into mine and she bit her lip. "I suck at this," she said and looked away.

"Eyes on me. Suck at what, Red?" At my words, she looked back at me.

"When we have sex... Well..."

"Am I not giving you something you need, Red? Tell me."

"No, no, it's just we go at each other. And don't get me wrong; I love fast and hard, even a little rough and slow, but with you, I want to know what it feels to..."

I pushed up to my hands holding myself away from her. "Goddammit, you can talk nasty, give as good as you get, but you can't just spit out what I'm not giving to you. Fuck, Red, what is it?" Her hands raised and she pushed at my chest to get me to move, but I wasn't going anywhere until she told me what the fuck was on her mind. "Say it!"

"You are such an asshole, Kaden. I was going to say that I wanted to know what it feels like to have slow and easy sex with someone you love, and that's why I wanted to start in the bed. I figured then we could christen the rest of the rooms with the hard and fast fucks we like so well."

My cocked had started to soften when I got pissed with Charlie stalling, but with her words, it was throbbing with the need to give her what she wanted.

"You love me, Red?"

"Yes. What did you think? I move in with guys just for mind-blowing sex!"

"You love me, *and* you think the sex is mind-blowing?"

"Ugh, get off me, Kaden."

"No." I went back to my elbows and used my hands to push her hair out of her face, then I cupped her face and looked into her eyes. "I love you, too, Red. And I am an asshole for not seeing to your needs." Charlie opened her mouth to speak, and I shook my head, stopping her. "I may not always remember to say the words to you, but know that when I look at you, hold you, or even get mad at you—that I do love you and I always will." As I spoke, I watched her eyes and they began to glisten with unshed tears.

"How can you come across as an asshole, then turn around and say the sweetest things?" she smiled, reached up, and caressed my cheek with her hand.

"Only with you. I want to give you everything."

"Oh, Kaden, you do. Don't ever doubt that. I have everything I need in you."

"You're already considered my ol' lady, but I want it all with you. Marry me, Red?"

"Yes," was all she got out before my mouth took hers. While I kissed her, I used my knees to spread her legs and then shifted to lay between them when she opened her legs wide to accept me. As my cock touched her entrance, I felt the wetness and began to push in painstakingly slow. I would show her gentle if it killed me.

Charlie moaned around my tongue when I was settled deep inside her. My tongue tasted every crevice of her mouth while I waited for her to adjust. Her hands ran through my hair and her fingers tried to make purchase with the short length. When she began to squirm, I broke the kiss and proceeded to move each of her arms above her head and held them both by the wrist in one hand while I used my other arm to keep me from squashing her into the mattress. I tightened my grip on her wrist to keep her from breaking free, knowing that if her hands touched me as I tried to give her what she wanted, it would be over before it began.

My cock pulsed against her walls as I slid in and out slowly. I could feel the pressure building in my sac, and I knew Charlie was close, too, as her pussy began to tighten around me. Charlie's eye never left mine as we went over the edge together.

I rolled until we laid on our sides and eased my cock from inside her. Charlie's head rested on my chest and I wrapped my arms around her.

"I love you so much, Kaden."

"I love you, too."

As her breathing evened out, I kissed the top of her head and closed my eyes. We could break in the other rooms when we woke up.

CM Books, LLC

Epilogue

Keg

Mac, another new prospect lifted his chin as I rode through the gate at Haven. A few members were outside when I parked, but that wasn't what caught my attention, it was the kid moving around looking at the bikes. I dismounted and walked to where the boy stood beside Crank's bike, admiring the dual chrome pipes. When I saw his hand reach out, I walked a little faster.

"Hey, be careful, those could still be hot," I said as I reached him.

"Is it yours?" the kid asked as he looked up at me. His face showed he was young; however, when he stood, he was tall and big for whatever his age was. His hair was dark brown and long enough that the one side fell across his face causing him to swing his head to get it out of his eyes.

"Nah, that is mine over there," I pointed toward my bike, "this one belongs to my brother, Crank. You like it?" I asked and saw the gleam in his brown eyes as he smiled.

201

"Yeah, it's freakin' sweet. The paint job on the gas tank is wicked, especially the skull. Did he buy the bike like that?"

I wanted to laugh at the excitement in his voice. I never saw him around the club before, so I knew he didn't belong to any of the members unless someone had family visiting that had never been here before.

"No. He bought the bike but added a few things to it and then had the tank painted."

"It is sweet," he said and bent over to get a better look at the Haven emblem painted on the side of the tank.

"You into bikes, huh?" I imagine the look on his face was the same one I had the first time I was around bikes.

"I'm trying to get my mom to buy me one so I can ride on the farm, but she says I'm not old enough. Christ, I'm twelve, not two."

I bit the inside of my cheek to keep from chuckling when I saw him roll his eyes. Damn, I didn't envy his mom and dad with the boy's attitude. I imagined he was a handful.

"What's your name, kid?" I asked as he continued to examine Crank's bike, checking every detail out.

"Ryker Allen. Everyone calls me Ry."

"Okay," I chuckled. "Bet you catch shit for that, don't you?" I asked because damn, his parents had to know what they were doing when they named him.

"At first, but now I just tell them my mom gave that name because my dad was serving time there when I was born," Ry smirked, and I laughed.

Smart kid.

"Nice. You here with your mom or your dad?"

"My mom. She's a vet. My little sister and I came with her so she could look at some snake. It's sick or something. She mostly works with regular animals or large animals like horses and cows. My sister went inside with her because she likes snakes."

"You don't?"

"Nah, they give me the creeps. I don't even like the black snakes that hang around the barn to eat the mice." Ry cringed.

"Yeah, I'm with you there, kid."

"Well, there she is, gotta go," Ry said and moved past me. I turned to follow so I could ask Freak about his pet. The man took better care of his snakes than he did himself.

Ry's mom was holding the hand of a little dark-haired girl while talking with a couple of the guys who were standing out front. She had her back to us. When we walked up, she and the little girl turned around—then I was left speechless as a piece of my past met my eyes.

CM Books, LLC

Acknowledgment

To my readers: May the New Year bring you happiness, good health, wealth, and lots of extra time for reading.

Carson

CM Books, LLC

CM Books, LLC

About the Author

Carson Mackenzie enjoys writing romance with a real feel inside the stories. She writes with the belief not every man is a jerk and not every woman needs saving.

Carson lives in the South with one of her sons, a Great Dane and two adopted shelter dogs that keep the household in line. Books have always been a part of her life. There is nothing better to her than curling up and relaxing with a good story and losing herself in someone else's world for a few hours.

Writing stories and growing as an author with each book is her goal. She wants to reach the level where a reader knows when they see her name, they can trust in the fact there will be a good story as they flip through the pages.

Carson's been her writing journey for a few years. As she's finally starting to settle in, her only regret is she hadn't started sooner.

Stay up to date with what I'm working on:

Webpage: www.carsonmackenzieauthor.com/
Goodreads:
www.goodreads.com/author/show/14764937.Carson_Mack enzie

CM Books, LLC

Books by Carson Mackenzie

Black Hawk MC

Speed
Crusher
Devil
Ghost
Jag
Coast
Flirt

Haven MC

Moose's Regret
Hawk's Bounty
Keg's Revelation

Desert Phoenix MC

Desert Phoenix Rising

CM Books, LLC

Standalones
Her Way or No Way
Two Paths One Destiny

CM Books, LLC

CM Books, LLC

www.ingramcontent.com/pod-product-compliance
Lightning Source LLC
Chambersburg PA
CBHW020412210626
46816CB00006BB/2240